Praise for *Because Your Vampire Said So*

"Lively, sexy, out-of-this-world—as well as in it— fun! Michele Bardsley's vampire stories rock!"
—*New York Times* Bestselling Author Carly Phillips

"I laughed nonstop from beginning to end.... Michele Bardsley always creates these characters that leave readers feeling like they are our next-door neighbors.... I've been addicted to these books since the very first one was written, but I have to say I think *Because Your Vampire Said So* is my favorite so far.... If I could, I'd give this story a higher rating. Five ribbons just don't seem to be enough for this wonderful story!"
—Romance Junkies

"An excellent addition to the Broken Heart series."
—Fresh Fiction

"Another Broken Heart denizen is here in this newest, hysterically funny first-person romp. The combination of sexy humor, sarcastic wit, and parental trauma is unmistakably Bardsley. Grab the popcorn and settle in for a seriously good time!"
—*Romantic Times*

"Funny, sassy, and sexy."
—*Rendezvous*

"Michele Bardsley has a wicked sense of humor.... After reading this book, all I can say is that I hope Michele Bard............ming. I can't wait to read about m.....................t."
............omance

continued ...

"Hysterically funny and surprisingly moving. . . . If you need a good laugh and want some feel-good fun . . . grab this series up and enjoy the hell out of it!"
—Errant Dreams

Praise for *Don't Talk Back to Your Vampire*

"Cutting-edge humor and a raw, seductive hero make *Don't Talk Back to Your Vampire* a yummylicious treat!"
—Dakota Cassidy, author of *The Accidental Werewolf*

"A fabulous combination of vampire lore, parental angst, romance, and mystery. I loved this book!"
—Jackie Kessler, author of *The Road to Hell*

"All I can say is *wow*! I was totally immersed in this story to the point that I tuned everything and everybody out the whole entire evening. Now that's what I call a good book. Michele can't write the next one fast enough for me!"
—The Best Reviews

"A winning follow-up to *I'm the Vampire, That's Why*, filled with humor, supernatural romance, and truly evil villains."
—*Booklist*

Praise for *I'm the Vampire, That's Why*

"From the first sentence, Michele grabbed me and didn't let me go! A vampire mom? PTA meetings? A sulky teenager? Throw in a gorgeous, ridiculously hot hero and you've got the paranormal romance of the year. Get this one *now*."
—MaryJanice Davidson

"Hot, hilarious, one helluva ride. . . . Michele Bardsley weaves a sexily delicious tale spun from the heart."
—L. A. Banks

Wait Till Your Vampire Gets Home

Michele Bardsley

A SIGNET ECLIPSE BOOK

SIGNET ECLIPSE
Published by New American Library, a division of
Penguin Group (USA) Inc., 375 Hudson Street,
New York, New York 10014, USA
Penguin Group (Canada), 90 Eglinton Avenue East, Suite 700, Toronto,
Ontario M4P 2Y3, Canada (a division of Pearson Penguin Canada Inc.)
Penguin Books Ltd., 80 Strand, London WC2R 0RL, England
Penguin Ireland, 25 St. Stephen's Green, Dublin 2,
Ireland (a division of Penguin Books Ltd.)
Penguin Group (Australia), 250 Camberwell Road, Camberwell, Victoria 3124,
Australia (a division of Pearson Australia Group Pty. Ltd.)
Penguin Books India Pvt. Ltd., 11 Community Centre, Panchsheel Park,
New Delhi - 110 017, India
Penguin Group (NZ), 67 Apollo Drive, Rosedale, North Shore 0632,
New Zealand (a division of Pearson New Zealand Ltd.)
Penguin Books (South Africa) (Pty.) Ltd., 24 Sturdee Avenue,
Rosebank, Johannesburg 2196, South Africa

Penguin Books Ltd., Registered Offices:
80 Strand, London WC2R 0RL, England

First published by Signet Eclipse, an imprint of New American Library,
a division of Penguin Group (USA) Inc.

First Printing, November 2008
10 9 8 7 6 5 4 3 2 1

To Renee Nagel, without whom this book would've never been written. Seriously. The next time you see her, thank her profusely for spending hours on the phone with me going over scenes, offering suggestions, and listening to me whine.

And to Terri Smythe and Dakota Cassidy, who also did their fair share of write-the-damn-book motivational speeches and hand-holding (when Renee was on break).

You three are the best hug-giving, sweet-talking, ass-kicking friends *evah*.

And to Sue Seeley, who has the best taste in paranormal fiction. Thanks for the love, darling.

ACKNOWLEDGMENTS

Thank you to all my readers. To those who send me emails and post comments, please know that I adore you even if you don't hear from me. Big, sloppy smooches to my Yahoo! Group: groups.yahoo.com/group/MicheleBardsley. You guys are the best!

I'm so lucky to have Stephanie Kip Rostan as my literary agent. How do I repay you for believing in me? Truly, there's not enough chocolate in the world. I also adore Monika "Terminator" Verma, who terrifies accountants on my behalf.

I appreciate my awesome editor, Kara Cesare, who always helps me write better books, and my fellow Track Changes nerd Lindsay Nouis.

I'm tremendously grateful to Kara Welsh, Claire Zion, and New American Library. The editorial staff, production crew, and cover artists *rule*. Thank you for all your hard work!

Chapter 1

I hugged the large oak tree as I tried to catch my breath. Sneaking around this creepy little town in the dark—and during winter, no less—was such a bad idea. Especially considering I'd been scared out of my wits by those . . . those *howls*.

Shivers raced up and down my spine. What in the world had made those terrifying sounds? Surely not dogs. Coyotes? Wolves? Eek! My shivering turned into full-body shudders.

"Crystal One, Crystal One," spat my cell phone. It was on two-way radio mode. "Please state your location."

My gloves were thick, but I managed to press the button on the phone's side. "Seriously, Mom," I whispered. "Do we have to use ridiculous code names?"

"I almost named you Crystal." Her tone suggested she'd always regretted that decision. Oh, please. Burdening an infant with "Seraphina Liberty Windsong Monroe" was bad enough. I started calling myself Libby at the age of ten, much to Mom's disappointment. However, my parents were all about free expression and independent thinking. If their only child desired to be called Libby, that desire would be honored.

"Crystal One?"

I rolled my eyes. "I'm here, Ruby Two. I'm still in the woods, but I can see the cemetery, so I'll head toward it. Where are you?"

"We're just off the main road, walking toward a place called the Thrifty Sip. It looks abandoned. Sapphire Three is lamenting his hoped-for ICEE."

I laughed. My dad's single dietary weakness was a frothy, sugary, colorful ICEE, which my mother equated to the devil's brew. Dad told me once that everyone needed to indulge in one bad-for-you thing. "Makes life worth living, Peanut," he'd said with a wink.

I clicked the button again. "Any signs of Bigfoot?"

"None," responded Mom. "But those howls sounded promising. Werewolves, maybe."

For the last few months, stories about Broken Heart, Oklahoma, had circulated among paranormal investigators. Everything from sightings of Bigfoot to tales of flying men had been bandied about until my parents could no longer resist the challenge. They'd spent the last twenty-five years trying to prove the existence of vampires, werewolves, Bigfoot, angels, aliens, other dimensions, and all kinds of supernatural phenomenon. In 1983 they started Paranormal Research and Investigation Services, aka PRIS. I was born two years later, and they'd raised me to believe in the paranormal.

We'd lived on the road, so I'd been homeschooled. My curriculum included Math, English, Astral Projection, and Psychic Phenomena. I got my GED, then I took the certificate course at the Institute of Transpersonal Psychology. After I finished the twelve-month program, I went to California and enrolled in the HCH Institute. Another year, another certificate—this one in Parapsychological Studies.

Getting those certificates wasn't nearly as much fun as slogging through the Louisiana swamps looking for Bayou Boo, half man and half alligator.

At the age of twenty-three, I was itching to strike out on my own. It wasn't that I didn't believe in my parents' dreams of discovering the unknown, or, in most cases, the unbelievable. I yearned for something all my own. I supposed it was time to create the life I wanted . . . only I didn't yet know what I wanted.

I tucked the phone into my coat pocket. We were supposed to meet back at the car in thirty minutes.

We'd been in Tulsa to check out a haunted hotel (nope, no ghosties), and decided to hit Broken Heart on the way to meet our team in Texas.

Ack! So. Freaking. Cold. And I was still unnerved by the animal cries. I listened for the howls, relieved when I heard nothing but the wind rattling the branches above me. Some investigator I was! I wasn't supposed to let little things like werewolves (ack!) and freezing weather stop me.

I pressed my cheek against the tree. No warmth there. Why hadn't I thought of a ski mask? The black parka had done a fair job of keeping most of me warm, but the hood offered no protection to my face. My skin felt scraped raw by the chilled air. The rough bark wasn't exactly helping, either.

I let go of the tree, but stayed close. I readjusted the strap of my oversized purse, which clunked in protest. My parents were big believers in being prepared and they'd taught me many skills. MacGyver had nothing on us.

I inhaled the loamy smell of earth and the crisp scent of pine. It felt like tiny icicles were forming in my nose and lungs. I heard some nearby rustling and clenched the oak, peering around the wide trunk.

I stifled a gasp when I saw a man kneeling next to a heart-shaped marble tombstone, which looked the worse for wear. The top right corner had broken off. He placed an armful of brightly colored silk flowers on the ground and appeared to be talking to the headstone.

Oh, crap. Spying on someone in a graveyard was so wrong. But I couldn't quite convince myself to walk away.

I was fairly close, but because my glasses were flotsam in the junk sea of my purse, I had to squint to read the inscription:

THERESE ROSEMARIE GENESSA
BELOVED WIFE AND MOTHER
1975–2006

He wasn't exactly dressed for cold weather. He wore white Nikes, jeans, and a thick, blue sweater. No coat, gloves, or hat. He looked like a normal guy. Nice bod, but not one made by Bowflex. Who knew? Maybe that sweater hid some rock-hard abs.

He took out a spade and started to work around the edge of the marble base.

The silence was ungodly. No chirping crickets, stir of little mammals, or twitter of birds. In this odd quiet, the spade rasped unpleasantly as the man thrust it into the hard-packed earth, alternating between scraping and digging.

Feeling more and more uncomfortable, I studied the rest of the cemetery. Tombstones were tilted, broken, or fallen. The place looked as if it had been ravaged by an earthquake. It looked old, but not uncared-for. I idly wondered what had happened to the place.

My gaze returned to the man. I really shouldn't get any closer, but I wasn't interested in retracing my steps. I might accidentally find the source of those hair-raising howls. He might not know it, but the guy tending the grave was the closest thing to safety I had right now.

About five feet away was a lone pine tree with thickly covered branches. I held my breath and initially tiptoed from my cover, eventually racing to the pine and ducking under its flagging limbs. The needles poked at me, so I scrunched down. I was near enough to see his determined expression. He had brown hair, cut short. A nice, friendly face. Not drop-dead gorgeous, but pleasant.

I crouched next to the tree and watched him make a narrow trench. Then he stuck the flowers in and arranged them. I don't know why I stayed. Watching a man do this heart-wrenching work wasn't exactly polite. I guess I just didn't want to leave. I felt like someone needed to stand watch with him, even if he was unaware of my presence. Stupid, right?

The wind kicked up, slicing at my face like Ginsu knives. I clamped my lips together to keep my teeth from chattering.

The man finished putting the flowers together,

scooped the dirt around 'em, and patted down the soil with the flat end of the spade.

He stared at the grave and I stared at him. Something about him niggled at me. His face was a shade too pale. I couldn't fault a guy who wasn't into baking his skin. No, it was his utter stillness that freaked me out.

"You can come out now." He stood up, dusted off his jeans, and turned his gaze directly to the pine tree. To *me*.

How had I given myself away? Even though moments earlier I'd thought of him as my safety net, I knew better than to just stroll out and introduce myself. I'd learned over the years that not everything was as it seemed. He looked nice and sounded nice, but hey, so did serial killers—right until they put a knife to your throat.

"You are not afraid. You will come to me," he said. His tone dropped an octave and went all seductive.

Yeah, right, Mr. Sexy Voice. I clutched the tree while my mind raced. Oh, to hell with it. I ducked out from underneath the unwieldy branches and raced toward the forest.

I heard the growls two seconds before I saw the animals issuing the threats. Two huge, pissed-off wolves raced toward me.

Ohmygodohmygodohmygod!

"Aaaaaaaaahhhh!" My scream echoed into the

dense forest. Heart thumping, stomach roiling, fear prickling, I made a U-turn and ran back the other way. The growls gave way to fierce barking.

I shot past the pine tree. He was still there! My grave-digging safety man! His puzzled expression switched to alarm. His eyes went wide and he dropped the spade, which was a good thing, because I launched myself at him.

He caught me, staggered backward, and then tried to let me go.

"Pick me up! Pick me up!" I screeched. "Save me already!"

Chapter 2

The man scooped me into his arms and held me close. I pressed my face into his shoulder and held on to him like he was Superman. I wished he *was* Superman—then he could fly me away from danger.

"Are th-they gone?" I asked. My purse dangled from my right side, slapping at my hip. "Did you s-scare them away?"

"No." His hands twitched underneath me. "Um . . . oh. You're . . . uh, breathing hard on my neck."

"So what?" I was *terrified*, and he was complaining about my breath control?

He swallowed heavily. "It's a sensitive spot."

"Here?" I asked, allowing my breath to roll over his skin again. *Why* was I asking him about the area

9

under his left ear? Knowing where not to breathe on him wasn't all that relevant.

"Hm-mmm." He sounded discombobulated.

Well, so was I. I lifted my head and glanced down. The wolves were a couple of feet away, pacing. Their fur was thick and glossy—shimmering like black silk in the moonlight.

"What are they doing?" I whispered.

"Deciding whether or not to eat you."

I squealed and tried to glue myself to . . . to . . . "Who are you?"

"Ralph Genessa. And you are?"

"Scared out of my freaking mind." I tightened my grip around his neck.

"That's an unusual name."

"Ha ha *ha*. Have you done Leno yet?"

His brows rose. Oh, right. My name. "I'm Libby Monroe."

The wolves snapped and snarled.

I screamed. Jamie Lee Curtis had nothing on me.

Ralph almost dropped me. He staggered back a few steps, his hands gripping me hard, but he managed to keep us both upright.

"Would you mind not doing that again?" he snapped. "They won't hurt us."

"You're an optimist, aren't you?" Death was three feet from us. *Stinky, slobbery death*. My heart tried to escape, first by trying to pound out of my chest, then by attempting to climb out of my throat.

The wolves continued to show their teeth and growl, but they didn't try to maul us. Why wouldn't they leave?

"Please, Ralph," I begged. "Make them go away."

"I'm not the Dog Whisperer."

"Jeez! Give it a whirl!"

He laughed.

Startled by this reaction, I peered up at him—and felt socked in the stomach. How could I have thought he was only pleasant-looking? That smile transformed his face, which would've given Brad Pitt a run for his money.

Despite our thick clothing, I could tell he wasn't soft and flabby, either. My rescuer was better built than I thought. His muscles flexed under my legs and back where he held me. An electric thrill zipped up my spine, which was far better than the fear still doing the jig in my stomach.

"Don't worry," he said.

"You're kidding, right?"

"I was talking to them," he clarified.

To them? To the *wolves*? Uh . . . why had I thought leaping into his arms was a good idea?

The wolves barked.

I squeaked and threw my arms around Ralph's neck. My purse smacked him on the back and he grunted.

"I'll take care of her," Ralph said. "If she doesn't kill me first."

They barked again.

"Yes, I'll call Patrick."

Who was Patrick? And why did he need to be called? I ventured another look down. The wolves stared at me, their teeth still showing in that we-will-devour-you-with-hot-sauce way, and then took off.

I looked at Ralph, stunned that he had somehow communicated with the animals. His blue eyes glittered with humor and with concern and . . . ooooooh, what was *that*? Interest? Of the sexual kind? My heart skipped a beat.

"What just happened here?"

He shrugged. "I gave it a whirl."

"Nice." Now that the wolves were gone, I felt a scooch more courageous. As a bonus, my heart decided to stay put and resume its normal beat.

"What are you doing here?" He sounded curious, which was far better than accusatory.

"My car broke down." The lie rolled off my tongue easily, even though my heart stuttered. I stared at him, trying not to look away. I hated telling fibs, but PRIS wasn't always welcomed with open arms. Some people thought we were a joke, and others a threat.

"You're a liar," he accused softly.

I couldn't stop my flinch. I averted my gaze, which probably just confirmed for him that he was right.

"What are you doing here, Libby Monroe?"

His voice did the sex-you-up thing again, and I found myself gazing deeply into his gorgeous blue eyes. What was with the Dracula tone and the come-hither glance?

"Tell me your purpose for coming to Broken Heart."

I couldn't look away from him. I swear there was a flare of red in his eyes. Fear flamed for an instant. No, no. My imagination had gotten the better of me.

"Not that I'm weirded out by it or anything, but why are you channeling Bela Lugosi?"

He looked surprised, then worried, and then uncertain. His confusion afforded me the opportunity to ask a question of my own.

"Who are the flowers for, Ralph?"

Oh, hell. Had I really just asked that? I felt as shocked as he looked. Hadn't I meant to quiz him about Bigfoot sightings? Maybe even cop to my real reason for snooping around Broken Heart?

Ralph dropped my legs, which thunked to the ground. Pain shimmied up my calves. As soon as my footing was secure, he let the rest of me go. My heavy purse nearly tipped me over. I righted myself, heaving the bag over my shoulder.

"Forgive me," I said, feeling guilty. "I shouldn't have asked."

"You're right. You shouldn't have spied on me, either."

"Yeah. That, too."

His lips thinned. Then, as if he was compelled to tell me, he said quietly, "Therese was my wife. She died three years ago."

"I'm sorry," I said, meaning it. I didn't say anything else because no words could really comfort the grief-stricken. When I was thirteen, my uncle Archie died during an investigation. An explosion killed him instantly. He wasn't really my uncle, just a key member of the PRIS team. But I'd known him my whole life and I missed him every day.

"C'mon, let's go." He sounded weary and resigned. Ralph pointed to a silver Honda, which was parked on the narrow road that cut through the cemetery. "Get in the car."

"No way." I unzipped my purse and felt around for my can of pepper spray. Vaguely, I recalled a tenet from my self-defense class: If someone tries to kidnap you, fight. Never go with them to a second location. The can rolled under my fingertips and I yanked it out, pointing the nozzle at his face. "Back off!"

"Two minutes ago, you begged me to save you." He studied the can. "Now you're threatening me with hair spray. And Aqua Net, no less. Does this look like the 1980s to you?"

"Shut up. It was on sale." I looked at the trial-sized can and grimaced. "Aqua Net stings, buddy. And it'll glue your eyes shut."

Ralph sighed.

"You know, just because—" I stopped, peering at

the copse of trees a few yards away. A strange man rounded a tree and shuffled toward us. He dragged one leg, his arms were crooked oddly, and his clothes were disheveled.

"Who is that?" I asked.

Ralph turned, took one look at the weirdo, then grabbed my arm and hustled me toward his car. I looked over my shoulder. The man hit a pocket of moonlight. His skin was flaking and gray, and his hair patchy. Worse, two sunken holes were where his eyes should've been.

I shrieked. Yanking my arm out of Ralph's grasp, I sprinted toward the car. I scrambled to the passenger side, flinging open the door. We both got inside and locked our doors. I watched the man move relentlessly, if slowly, toward the Honda.

"What is that thing?" I asked, my voice shaking.

"Zombie." Ralph started the car and put it in gear. I dropped my purse on the floor and clutched my hair spray can. I felt cold and it wasn't because of the weather. My whole body trembled.

Thwump!

Something heavy landed on the roof. I looked up and saw indentations. What could crush metal that easily?

Ralph slammed his foot on the gas. The car shot forward, but our rooftop companion was not tossed off.

Whatever-it-was leapt onto the hood and faced

us. The man crouched down, his fingers hooked into the gap between the windshield and the hood. Sickly pale. Ragged clothes. Bloodred eyes.

"Okay. Who is *that*?" I asked, my voice rising in panic.

"Vampire," said Ralph.

Right. Vampire. Ooookay.

I almost preferred the zombie.

The road curved to the right, but Ralph missed the turn. The Honda darted across the grass and spun through a row of graves before he managed to get back on the road.

"Why don't you hit the brakes? He'll go flying!"

The man punched the windshield, shattering the glass. He ripped the whole window out and flung it away. Shards scattered across the dash, into the floor, and on my lap.

Ralph slammed the brakes hard.

The car died.

Worse, our nemesis did not go flying. Jeez! Was he superglued to the hood?

His insane gaze ravenous, the vampire (no, really?) reached for me like I was a juicy steak. His grin revealed blackened teeth and sharp fangs. I stared at his mouth, horrified.

"Libby!"

Ralph's shocked cry shook me out of my numbness. I aimed the Aqua Net and sprayed the dude. He yelled and clawed at his eyes.

I dug around in my purse until I found the object I wanted.

I held up the candle lighter, clicked on the flame, and sprayed the Aqua Net. Flames shot forward and encompassed the man's grimy hands, which were still pressed against his face. His greasy hair was instantly flambéed.

He fell off the car and rolled around on the ground.

Ralph kept trying to start the car, but the engine refused to turn over. The vampire was still yowling and cursing. Ew. He smelled like burning mold.

I heard a long, low moan and looked over my shoulder. Through the back window, I saw the zombie shuffling toward us.

Hysteria burst through me. What was going on in this town? Killer wolves, zombies, and vampires. . . . *Jeez!*

Ralph shoved his door open. He looked at me over his shoulder. "What are you waiting for?" he yelled. "Run!"

Chapter 3

I scrambled across the seats and out the driver's side door. Ralph grabbed my hand and we took off. He ran faster and faster, and soon I couldn't keep up. My hand slipped out of his as he sped toward the main road.

My heart pounded wildly and my legs ached. I slowed to a walk, and gulped in cold air that did little to get oxygen into my burning lungs.

"What are you doing?"

"Aaaaaahhhh!" I stumbled back and glared at Ralph. A minute ago, he was at least twenty yards away. Now he was standing in front of me, his blue eyes filled with impatience.

"How did you do that?" I asked. "You should try out for the Olympics."

"Watch out!" He grabbed my arm and yanked me forward.

I went sailing through the air. Ralph didn't know his own strength. I landed a couple of feet away and collapsed to my knees. My purse fell off my shoulder and spilled its contents. As I picked up all the objects, fear battered at me. I sucked in a steadying breath.

Okay. If I were to believe my eyes and twenty-three years of parental insistence, then I'd just met my first zombie and vampire. Broken Heart was paranormal central. Was that guy who'd jumped on the hood really a vampire?

I was starting to freak out.

"Om mani padme hum." I drew the syllables out like I'd been taught to do. Chanting was as automatic to me as breathing. "Om mani padme hum."

I repeated the mantra as I shoved keys, coin purse, lighter—*oh, there's the pepper spray*—gum, magnifying glass, pocket dictionary, and Sharpie into my bag. By the time I finished, I felt more in control.

I zipped up my purse and got to my feet. I pulled my cell phone out of my pocket and hit the button. "Mom? I mean, Ruby Two?"

No response. I pushed the button again. "Hey! Ruby Two! Sapphire Three! You there?"

Neither Mom nor Dad picked up. Panic fluttered

again. I had to get to the Thrifty Sip. I had to find my parents.

I turned around. Oh, crap. Ralph was fighting the . . . uh, vampire. And he was losing. The creep had him on the ground, his hands around Ralph's throat.

Ralph kept punching him, but the man didn't budge. Heck, he didn't even flinch.

"The cure!" he rasped. "I want the cure!"

Ralph gurgled.

Terror was too mundane a word to describe how I felt. Knees wobbling and stomach churning, I marched over and whapped the assailant upside the head with my purse.

He yowled. The distraction was enough for Ralph to get the upper hand. But he needn't have bothered. The vampire leapt off Ralph and grabbed me. With one hand clenched on my coat, he hoisted me off the ground and hissed.

Oh my God! My feet dangled as I stared at him in shock. Even though I had set fire to his face, the damage was minute. I gaped at him, staring at his fangs.

He jerked the purse out of my flaccid hands and threw it over my head. Then he pulled me down until my face was a mere inch from his. His rank breath feathered my lips. Ugh.

"You smell delicious."

I screamed. I was seriously starting to feel like a heroine trapped in a horror movie.

"Let her go!" Ralph wrapped his arm around the vampire's neck and pulled back hard. The vampire's red-tinged eyes went wide as he made squeak-cough sounds.

He didn't release me. Those pale, thin fingers were embedded in my coat. He wasn't going to let go.

Neither, apparently, was Ralph.

We engaged in an awkward dance. Ralph kept squeezing on the guy's neck while hitting him in the back. I rained blows on his shoulders, which had no effect other than making me feel better. I kicked him, too, but my flailing feet didn't inflict any damage. This guy was made out of stone.

A deep, haunting moan arrived just seconds before the zombie's big, gray hand landed on top of the bad guy's head. We all stopped fussing and turned to look at the fourth party that had joined our gruesome threesome.

"Hiiiii," said the zombie. "Saaaaave yooooou."

He grinned at me. At least I think he did. His mouth was mostly gone so it was hard to tell. Some of his teeth were missing, and those left were black and rotting. His breath was worse than the fanged guy's. I breathed through my mouth, but the stench still made my eyes water.

The zombie twisted the vampire's head. I heard bones snapping. Oh, now really. Yuckyuckyuck!

To save his own hide, the man let me go. But he didn't just drop me. The bastard threw me.

"Libby!" cried Ralph.

Once again, I found myself airborne, only much higher and faster. I let my body go completely limp. I hit the ground on my back, flopping onto the hard-packed earth like a rag doll.

For a moment, I imagined I was lying on the softest bedding in the world. I focused on the pearlescent moon perched in the black-velvet sky and breathed deeply. I assessed my body and, though it ached, I was glad I hadn't broken any bones.

Thank you, Yogini Shivali. Ten years of yoga lessons had paid off. Whew. I closed my eyes and took several more deep breaths.

"Oh my God! Libby!" Ralph's voice startled the hell out of me.

My eyes flew open and I looked directly into his concerned gaze. "Seriously. You should try out for the Olympics."

"You're okay?" His hands traveled over my arms and ribs, and then fluttered over my hips. His fingers lingered a smidge too long there, and my happy spot perked up. "Whoa there, bucko."

He chuckled as his hands tested my thighs, calves, and ankles. "Nothing broken."

"Yeah. Like you'd know."

"I would know," he said. "I was studying to be a paramedic before . . . well, before."

His wife died. Had his dreams died with her, too?

Gah! What was wrong with me? My thoughts seemed to go all mushy around this guy.

Ralph helped me sit up. I felt shaky and cold. I really wanted to go back to the hotel and forget tonight ever happened. So what if the proof that validated the existence of PRIS and my parents' life-long dreams had been chasing me around a cemetery?

Ralph's hands took mine and, though they weren't warm, I still felt heat tingle through me.

Well, maybe I didn't want to forget *everything*.

Ralph helped me to my feet and we looked at each other for a long moment. Every nerve ending prickled in anticipation. I saw Ralph's gaze dip to my mouth, and my ever-so-subtle response was to lick my lips.

"Hiiiii," said the zombie.

I nearly jumped out of my skin. "Jeez! Would you people stop sneaking up on me?"

We turned and looked at our unexpected friend. He dragged the vampire by his leg. The guy wasn't protesting much. I looked down and saw that his head had been turned 180 degrees. Had he been alive, he'd be staring at his own ass. He'd be eating a lot of dirt, too.

"Mm-mmph-mmph."

Neither Ralph nor the zombie had spoken.

"Mm-mmph-mmph!"

"What's that noise?" I asked.

The zombie dropped the pant leg clutched in his gray fist and leaned down to roll the dead guy over. It was really weird to see a head on the wrong side of its body. Believe it or not, that wasn't the weirdest part.

The man glared at us balefully. He spit out grass and dirt. "Like it's not bad enough I have the Taint," he rasped. "Everyone says the cure's in Broken Heart. I want it!" He paused. "By the way, this isn't comfortable."

"H-he's alive." I thought I had accepted that he was a vampire. I mean, the fangs, and the jumping on moving cars, and the talking with a twisted neck . . . yep, all that added up to vampire.

"Yeah, he's alive," said Ralph, grimacing. "The only way to kill him is to sever the head completely."

"Oh." I really didn't want to see someone get decapitated. "You'd think he wouldn't be able to talk since his throat is messed up."

"Good point." Ralph studied my face. "Are you okay?"

"Yeah, yeah. I'm good," I lied. I felt as though I was slowly spinning. Cold tingles welled up from my stomach and washed over me. I jerked a thumb at the gray-skinned, eyeless corpse. "He's really a zombie."

"I'm afraid so."

"Why did we run away from him? He seems nice, even if he is a walking corpse."

Ralph shrugged. "He just really geeks me out."

"Totally. Um . . . and that other guy should be dead."

"He's already dead," said Ralph. He sighed. "He's a vampire."

"Right." Nausea roiled. Dizziness overwhelmed me.

"Libby?" He stepped forward. "You look pale."

"You should talk," I mumbled. Suddenly suspicious, I looked him over. "Oh, don't tell me. Are you a vampire, too?"

"Yes," he admitted.

No way. I had hit the paranormal jackpot and I didn't know what to do. My parents were gonna flip! Unless they'd run into their own preternatural problems, and that's why they hadn't answered my call.

"I need to get to the Thrifty Sip."

Ralph's eyebrows winged upward. "It's closed."

"Just tell me where it is." I pulled out my phone. "I have GPS."

"In case you haven't noticed," he said, "we have bigger problems."

"Bigger than you think," gasped the prone vampire. "Heads up."

We immediately looked up.

Two large, winged monsters barreled out of the sky.

And they were on fire.

Chapter 4

"Holy shit!" shouted Ralph. He scooped me into his arms and took off like a shot. Before I knew it, we were safely on the road that Ralph had been aiming for when the car died. We were far enough away to be out of danger, but close enough to watch the action. He put me down and lucky, lucky me . . . he kept his arm around my shoulders.

I won't say anything about how nice his arm felt or how warm fuzzies turned into dancing butterflies in my belly. Because, y'know, that would be wrong. My timing always did suck.

We turned to watch the fiery creatures. They plowed into the earth, screeching and burning, like two huge, jeweled meteors. Dirt and grass exploded. The ground under our feet shook. We wobbled and held on to each other to keep upright.

I might as well say it: Dragons. Yep. And they landed on the zombie and the vampire.

"Oh. Ouch." I flinched. "Do you think . . ."

"No," said Ralph, answering the question I couldn't quite ask. "They're toast."

"Maybe squished by dragons should be added to the list of ways to kill vampires." It was inane to say, I admit, but I was tired of screaming. My throat hurt. And if I was trying to appear cool under pressure and failing miserably, so what?

"Noted," said Ralph. "Beheading, intense light, and dragon squishing. Bad for vamps."

I bit my lip because I wanted to laugh, and it was sooooo not the time to exhibit a sense of humor. I mean, really, who laughs at a time like this? Not me. No, sirree.

I gazed up at Ralph, but he looked all stoic and cute. He had a nice jaw. A little cleft in his chin. A thick fringe of lashes that so nicely framed his baby blues. Why did guys always get the great lashes?

My ruminations were cut short because Ralph gathered his wits before I did. He whipped out a cell phone and made a call. I took the cell out of my coat pocket and tried to call my parents, but with no luck. Worry gnawed at me; I pushed it away. We'd gotten out of a lot of jams over the years. If anyone was good at surviving peril, it was Dora and Elmore Monroe.

The dragons kept breathing fire on each other

and slashing at each other with sharp, black talons. One dragon was blue-green, and the other orange-red. The only positive thing about their battle was that their fire turned the freezing February air darn near tropic.

"Does this happen a lot?" I asked.

"Um . . . no. Not really." He squeezed me in a very nice (oh, baby!) hug. Then he seemed to realize what he'd done and let me go like *I* was on fire. He cleared his throat. "Don't worry. Help is on the way."

Uh, yeah. What kind of help could possibly resolve two dragons duking it out? I couldn't see Broken Heart cops showing up and hauling them off to jail.

"Oh! My purse!" My bag was just a few feet away. Wow. That vampire had lobbed it a huge distance. It had landed upright and, hey, no spillage. I ran toward it, thinking only about scooping it up. It had a lot of stuff inside, stuff I used and needed and didn't want to accumulate all over again.

"Libby!"

I didn't heed the warning in Ralph's voice because I had my eyes on the prize. I crouched near a headstone and reached for the strap.

ROOOOOOAAAAAR!

The orange-red dragon flew over me, its belly so close I could see the intricate pattern of its glistening scales. Its wing tip brushed my head.

Heart pounding and adrenaline spiking, I grabbed my purse and flattened to the grass.

The dragon landed on its side. The ground rolled underneath me, then shook violently. I squeezed my eyes shut and curled into a protective ball.

"Help me," cried a female voice.

I opened one eye. A couple of yards away lay a woman whom I can only describe as a dragon-woman. Her body was covered in a strange, shimmery material, which gleamed orange and red. Black liquid streaked her abdomen and chest. She coughed and the same liquid burbled from her lips.

Oh, God.

"Please," she cried. Desperation and pain filled her gaze.

The last thing I wanted to do was get anywhere near her. I wasn't a genius, but even I could figure out that she'd been the orange dragon. I'd studied shape-shifters. Rare was the mention of a were-dragon. And yet there she was, begging for my help.

Ruby Two and Sapphire Three would be really disappointed in me if I failed to help any living creature in trouble.

With the purse strap clenched in my fist, I rolled to my hands and knees. Where was the other dragon? Where was Ralph? Where was my common sense?

Ralph zipped past us, leaping over the injured

woman. He aimed both palms at the sky. Fire erupted. Ralph made hand motions and the fire shaped into large spheres.

I couldn't wrap my brain around this new development. Ralph was a vampire who could wield fire? Wasn't that an odd ability for a creature deathly allergic to all things light?

I didn't really have much time to ponder the question. Apparently a dragon could be as quiet as a stealth bomber. The blue-green soared toward us, soundless, its maw opening as flames licked its teeth. My heart leapt into my throat and I nearly choked.

The fire bombs struck it in the mouth, the chin, and the neck. Ralph relentlessly threw the fire at the creature. It flew higher into the sky, obviously pissed, trying to get out of range. Throwing fire at a dragon didn't seem all that smart. After all, dragons were fireproof. Maybe vampire fire was different. The blue dragon didn't seem to like it much.

I reached the girl. Up close, I could see her injuries were bad. Her odd skin had slashes from legs to shoulders, and several wounds were so deep I could see muscle and bone. My gorge rose. No. I had to keep it together. I could freak out later.

"What can I do?" I unzipped my purse and took out my box of wet wipes. I dabbed her face, wiped off her mouth, scrubbed her neck.

"Please." Her voice was a mere whisper.

From a side pocket, I pulled out my half-drunk bottle of Mountain Dew, my own little gustatory sin. I was a vegan. But that didn't mean I was immune to the sensual delights of junk food.

"I'm sorry." Tears crowded my eyes. God, I felt so helpless. She had to be in a lot of pain. "It's all I have. I promise I don't have cooties."

She smiled and I raised the bottle of soda to her mouth. She drank some, but it took effort.

I could hear Ralph's shouts, the constant roar of fire, and the growls of the blue dragon. Their battle continued, but I feared this woman's was over.

"No more time." She grasped my jacket with her long, orange fingers. Her red nails pierced the material. "My brother must not get my powers." She pulled me closer. "Kiss me."

"Oh. Uh . . . " I was all for granting last requests, but kissing a girl? "I'm really sorry. I'm not a lesbian."

Her laugh was hoarse. "I promise I don't have cooties."

She yanked me down and clamped her mouth on mine. The first thought that entered my mind was "No tongue!" The next thought was "Seriously! No tongue!" And then I realized the kiss wasn't a kiss. There was nothing sexual about it.

Fire shot from her mouth to mine. It roared through me, licking my skin, enveloping my insides. I tried to pull away, but we were sealed together. I felt her fingertips against my temples. God, it was so hot. Not porno hot. Falling-into-the-sun hot.

I was burning, burning.

"Libby!"

Ralph's voice sounded far away. I couldn't respond. I couldn't do anything but accept the fiery gift of the dragon.

Then it was over.

She collapsed to the ground, her hands falling away from my face. I knelt next to her, shivering, trying to draw in breath. Energy pulsed at the base of my spine, and spun a web of throbbing heat to every nerve ending. It was almost as if my blood had been burned away, leaving only the cleansing magical fire racing through my veins.

Streaks of red and orange blurred my vision.

My stomach rebelled and I fell to my side, vomiting black liquid.

What had she done to me?

"Libby!"

My vision cleared and I saw Ralph's legs. His white sneakers were battered and muddy. He squatted next to me, avoiding my puddle of ick, and helped me sit up.

"Jesus," he muttered. He grabbed the box of wipes and yanked one out. He cleaned my face, but the swipes were painful. Every inch of me felt raw, exposed. "What did she do to you?"

I gripped his wrist and he stopped wiping my cheeks.

"The . . . other . . . dragon," I managed to whisper.

"As soon as you and the other woman went inferno, the blue one took off."

"How . . . is . . . she?"

"She's gone, honey," he said gently. "Whatever she did to you, it was her last act on this Earth."

Some act. Where before it had felt like lava pouring through me, now it was as though I had been submersed in an Arctic sea. My teeth chattered and my vision grayed. I felt like I was sinking under the inky black of the cold ocean. Drowning in it.

I grabbed Ralph by the arms. "My . . . p-parents."

"We'll find them. I promise." He pressed his lips against my forehead. Electricity arced between us. Ralph was thrust away from me, his body writhing in orange-red flames.

I reached for him, tried to call his name.

My traitorous eyes closed and I unwillingly sank into the beckoning dark.

Chapter 5

My eyes fluttered open, though I wasn't quite able to focus them. After a while I was able to ascertain my surroundings. I lay on a soft surface and stared at a white vaulted ceiling. A very large chandelier—an exuberant explosion of shiny glass and chained gold—hung from the center beam. It had not been turned on, so it wasn't the source of the light in the room. I heard the crackling of fire and smelled cedar. It was weird, but I swear I could taste the soot.

It hurt to move. It hurt to breathe. Every muscle ached. My skin felt like it had been peeled off and glued back on. Even moving my eyebrows caused pain. I tried to sit up, but the whole world spun. I settled for leaning on my elbows, which also freaking hurt.

I reclined on a fancy velvet couch, probably an antique. My coat, gloves, and shoes had been removed and my purse was nowhere in sight. The lushly decorated room favored creams and burgundies and dark woods, but the oversized stone fireplace was its jewel.

A fire burned brightly inside it. I watched the flames undulate. I wanted to be closer. No, not closer. Inside. Warmth and safety could be found in fire.

Wait a minute. *What?* Building a cozy spot inside a fire was *bad*. Still, the flames were mesmerizing. Their heat, their dancing, their song.

Sheesh. I must've really hit my head hard. I lay back down and closed my eyes again. I took deep breaths, trying to find a calm spot in my roiling thoughts.

"Is she awake yet?" asked an Irish-tinged voice.

My eyes flew open. I was startled to see two men with shoulder-length black hair, mercury gazes, and the same faces leaning over me. Their expressions of curiosity were the same, too. Strangest of all was the pulsing color around them. One was outlined in blue, and the other in purple.

"Uh . . . hello," I said. I stared at the pulsing color. I knew about auras, of course. But these were solid, unchanging. And they smelled sweetly fetid, like dying roses.

"You feelin' all right?" asked the one on the left.

Are you kidding? I attempted a smile. "My head feels like a wet sandbag."

Questions crowded my mind and at the forefront: Where were my parents?

Had we really stumbled upon a town full of paranormal beings? What had that dragon girl done to me? And what the hell had happened to Ralph?

"My name is Patrick." He was the one on the left.

The guy on the right said, "I'm Lorcan."

"I'm Libby."

We all looked each other over for a few seconds. Then Lorcan grasped my hands and helped me to sit up.

Bad idea.

I swayed too far to the left. Patrick grabbed my shoulders and righted me. My stomach gurgled.

"I feel like I'm gonna yark."

Alarm flashed in his eyes. His gaze skidded to his brother, who had the same expression. I would've laughed except that I really did feel like vomiting. Yech.

I put my head between my knees and inhaled.

When my stomach settled, I slowly raised my head. *Deep breaths, Libby. Really deep breaths.* "How did I get here?"

"We found you at the cemetery," said Patrick. Or was it Lorcan? "Our doctor examined you, and said you had no major injuries and would be fine."

Then why didn't I feel fine? And what was with my sudden ability to see auras?

"What about Ralph?" I asked. "Is he okay? He sorta looked like he was on fire. But I was passing out at the time so I could be wrong."

"He's getting checked out now," said the man nearest me. "Was there anyone else?"

I hesitated. I didn't want to give away more information than necessary, especially to people who had yet to make clear their intentions. I decided not to mention my parents.

"There was a zombie. And an injured vampire." I made diving motions with my hands. "They were flattened by a couple of dueling dragons."

God, that sounded sooooo insane, but these two didn't blink.

"The woman who died," I continued. "She was a dragon."

"We didn't find a woman. Or a dragon," said the twin on the left. How had I already gotten them confused? An ache throbbed behind my eyes. At least my body no longer felt like someone was taking a cheese grater to it.

"Don't worry, Libby. We'll figure things out." The reassurance came from . . . Lorcan. Yeah. I was fairly sure the one sitting on the couch with me was Lorcan.

"Great. Then there's no reason for me to stick

around. Nice to meet you and everything. If you'll just hand over my stuff, I'll be on my way."

"To where?" asked Patrick. He folded his arms across his broad chest and smiled in a not-very-reassuring way.

"Away from here," I said decisively. "Wherever here is."

"You're being evasive," he accused.

"So are you."

"In what way?"

I rolled my eyes.

"Do you feel well enough to go on a little walk?" asked Lorcan.

I narrowed my eyes. "What kind of walk?"

He held up his hands in a surrender gesture. "Just upstairs."

"Why should I go up there?"

"Our queen has requested an audience," said Lorcan. His silver eyes flashed with amusement. "I think you'll find her quite refreshing."

"What exactly is she queen of?" I asked suspiciously.

"Depends on who you ask," answered Lorcan. "Suffice it to say, we consider her leadership valid."

Gee, that cleared everything up. "And what are you?"

Amusement flared again in his gaze; then those orbs went red and he showed me a big, fangy grin.

Even though I had already met two bloodsuckers, my heart still skipped a fearful beat. "Sheesh. You could've just said you were a vampire."

"Where's the fun in that?" His tone held restrained laughter. Well. I'm glad one of us was having a good time at my expense.

"Are you mental?" I asked, annoyed.

His raven eyebrows winged upward.

Patrick chuckled. "I'll take her to Patsy. Go on back to the compound."

Lorcan nodded and got up from the couch. He winked at me, then—poof! He disappeared in a shower of gold sparkles. He was gone, and I wished I knew how he'd pulled that magic trick. Then I could go poof, too.

"You know," I said conversationally, "if I hadn't already met a zombie, vampires, monster wolves, and a dragon, that would've been really impressive."

Patrick grinned.

The staircase looked as though Scarlett O'Hara would sweep down it any moment and declare, "After all . . . tomorrow is another day." It was wide, made of dark, polished wood, and curved as it rose upward. It had approximately four million steps.

After we got to the second floor, we walked along the hallway, our footsteps quieted by a thick carpet that was a faded burgundy. The walls looked freshly painted, a rather nice rose color with a chair rail that matched the wood of the staircase.

The hallway seemed to go on forever, but we finally reached the end and stopped in front of double doors, which were slightly ajar.

Patrick held my arm in a loose grip. I had stumbled several times and he probably thought I was going to keel over. I had no illusions I could escape, mostly because I still felt weak and more than a little shaky. I was worried about my parents. And my thoughts kept straying to Ralph. Was he okay? Were these his friends? What had happened to us in the cemetery?

I wasn't sure I wanted to meet the queen of this crazy freaking town. Nerves plucked at my stomach. I wondered where the queen fell on the bad-ass scale: Was she Cinderella-stepmom scary or off-with-her-head Queen of Hearts terrifying?

I looked at Patrick. "Um . . . should I curtsy or something?"

He smirked. "Yes. And always address her as 'most royal grand potentate.'"

"Seriously?"

"You don't want to know what happened to the last person who messed up the formal address." He slashed a line across his throat.

Oh, shit.

"Zerina, you have to stop changing people's hair

41

color." A woman's irritated voice filtered through the slight gap between the doors.

"I don't know what she's complaining about," answered a woman with a thick British accent. "Terran looks better with blue hair."

"Just stop doing it. Don't make me throw your skinny ass out the window."

Patrick knocked, then shoved open the doors. Shocked, I stood there like an idiot, gaping. He tugged on my arm and I followed him inside.

Three people stood in a large room obviously under construction. A single floor lamp offered me a limited view of the shadowy space. Tarps lay over furniture and scaffolding went to the vaulted ceiling. The sharp smell of fresh paint assailed me.

The woman in the middle was tall, blond, curvy, and gorgeous. She wore a dress that showed off the slight roundness of her pregnant belly. Next to her was a man built like a Greek god, his moon white hair pulled into a ponytail. They both had purple light emanating from them. I couldn't quite discern the scent; it was close to the spicy earth smell of sandalwood.

On the other side of the blonde was a petite woman, maybe in her twenties, with neon pink hair. She wore a black bustier, miniskirt, and thigh-high stockings. Her vinyl shoes were the same shocking pink as her hair. Whoa. Her eyes were pink, too. No surprise; her aura was sparkly pink and it smelled like cotton candy. She looked me over and found me boring.

Patrick, who wasn't exactly my friend to begin with, left me stumbling in his wake. He stopped short of the small gathering and jerked his head toward the blonde. Oh. The queen.

I attempted to curtsy, but my legs buckled and I dropped to my knees. I wasn't sure where to put my gaze. Hadn't I read you weren't supposed to look royalty in the eyes?

"Greetings, most royal . . ." Crap. What came next? "Wait. I'll get it. Uh . . . your most royal grand poot-n-toot. I mean, impotent." I sucked in a breath. After all I'd survived since arriving in Broken Heart, I was gonna die at the hands of a queen who demanded verbal tribute. "Your most royal grand potato head."

Silence was thick. My heart pounded and my whole body felt clammy. I looked up and saw Patsy's mouth open. *Cut off her head,* she'd scream manically.

"Potentate!" I yelled. "Your most magnificent royal grand on high potentate!"

Everyone burst out laughing.

What the hell was going on?

"Get up, honey," said the queen. "Patrick, you are such an asshole. You scared the crap out of her."

I got up, feeling light-headed. Relief poured

through me, but underneath squirmed embarrassment. I glared at an unrepentant Patrick.

The pink-haired woman grinned. "You looked like you pissed yourself."

I couldn't formulate a response to that comment.

"Don't worry," she went on. "I'm all for a little vengeance."

She flicked her fingers at Patrick's head. His beautiful, dark hair turned neon green.

"Zee!" yelled the blonde.

Zee laughed as she scurried out of the room.

I gaped at Patrick. "What—"

"She's a fairy."

"Oh." A fairy. Why the hell not? I sidled a look at Patrick's hair.

He sighed. "What does it look like this time?"

"Um . . . like Las Vegas threw up."

The blonde laughed. She looked me over, her expression friendly and curious. The man also studied me, his eyes an odd golden color. His nostrils flared almost as if he were scenting me. He didn't look quite as friendly.

She held out her hand and I shook it.

"I'm Patsy. And this is my husband, Gabriel."

"Libby Monroe."

Her husband didn't offer his hand, which was fine with me. I had no plans to get chummy with anyone except Ralph. Wait. No. Not even Ralph. Lick-alicious or not, he was still a vampire—one who could shoot fire from his hands. I don't even know how that was possible. Vampires weren't really my specialty. I was more a Bigfoot, Swamp Thing, Moth Man kind of girl. Maybe I should've read Mom's books. God knows she'd published enough of them.

Patsy turned to Patrick. "I feel weird about taking over the mansion."

"This place is the largest in town . . . fit for a queen," said Patrick, smiling. "Living in the house on Sanderson Street is a better fit for us. The Wiccans cleansed the whole house—which Jessica is now redecorating."

Patsy's eyebrows rose. "Why don't we go sit down?"

"But I was already sitting down," I whined. I was so frazzled, damn it. I pointed at Patrick, like he was an errant older brother. "He made me come up here."

"You're a poot, Patrick." Patsy laughed. "Stan's bringing over Ralph. He checked out okay." She wagged her finger at Patrick. "Take the girl down the easy way. We'll meet you in the living room."

Gabriel whispered in her ear and she rolled her eyes.

"How many do we have?" she asked.

"Three downstairs," said Gabriel. His lips twitched as if he might smile.

"Why do we need three living rooms?" groused

Patsy. "I swear to God, the whole town could live in this one house. Take her to the one y'all were in before, okay?"

Patrick wrapped his arms around my neck and brought me flush against him, which totally geeked me out. "What are you doing?"

"Taking you downstairs the easy way." He looked down at me. "Ready?"

"For wha—"

Chapter 6

"—at!" I sucked in a breath. "Shit! Oh, shit!"

My entire being had imploded and been reassembled in the blink of an eye. I was nauseated again.

Patrick let me go, but I grabbed him by the shirt and glared directly into his eyes. "Never, *ever* do that again!"

"It takes a while to get used to." He looked down at the white-knuckled grip I had on his threads. "You're ruining my favorite shirt."

I unclenched my fingers, then wobbled to the couch closest to the hearth. The fire made me feel better. Its warmth spread through me and gentled the roar in my head.

I heard singing.

I'd never heard anything like it in my life. It was a crystalline harmony.

"What kind of music is that?" I asked. They made me breathless, those delightful sounds.

"What music?" asked Patrick.

"You don't hear it?"

He shrugged, but his gaze said, *I only hear the ravings of a crazy person.*

Patsy and Gabriel came in, walking through the door like normal people. I guess they didn't feel it necessary to rearrange their atoms to get from one place to the next.

Patsy chose the divan opposite mine. Gabriel sat next to his wife. Patrick moved to the right side of the fireplace, leaning against the flat stone.

"Let's start from the beginning," said Patsy. "What were you doing in the cemetery?"

I didn't see the point in lying. I wasn't exactly a prisoner, but I doubted very much they'd let me walk out. At least not yet. I wondered if they had my parents somewhere else and, if they did, why hadn't they told me? Or brought them here, too? And if they didn't . . . my heart squeezed. But a dark little voice whispered that something was wrong. They were in danger.

For all I knew, so was I.

"I'm with PRIS," I admitted.

Patsy and Gabriel looked at me blankly, but Patrick's interest was piqued. He shifted toward me, his gaze intense. "Paranormal Research and Investigation Services has a team in Oklahoma?"

"Yes," I said, unnerved by his intensity. "Relax, dude. We're not a hit squad. We only investigate the paranormal."

"Sweet Lord," murmured Patsy. "You certainly hit jackpot, didn't you?"

"The Megabucks. We've gotten evidence here and there, but nothing big enough to shut up the skeptics." I glanced at her. "Nothing like this."

"PRIS and other such organizations cause problems for us," said Patrick. "The world is not ready for us. When it's time to integrate, we'll do so on our own terms."

Patsy held up her hand to stall Patrick's next words. "Save the lecture. We have a lot more to do before worrying about taking those steps." With a loud sigh she looked to my right, where no one sat. "Quit nattering. Who are you?"

Sheesh. The queen had a short memory. "Er . . . Libby Monroe."

Her gaze flicked to mine. "Sorry, hon. I wasn't talking to you." She stared at the blank space next to me for a minute. Then she said, "Thanks, Melvin. Yes, I'll tell her. Ew. No. You can't do that without lips."

No one else in the room seemed to find her behavior odd. Hey, I knew when to shut up. I tried to appear nonchalant, but it was hard to keep my gaze off Patsy.

"Melvin says he saved you from the Tainted vampire."

"Huh?"

"Melvin was the zombie." Patsy grimaced. "I never have figured out how his soul found its way back into his corporeal form. He's been hanging around the cemetery, annoying everyone." Her head swiveled to the blank spot and her mouth dropped. "Holy crap. Did a dragon really squish Melvin?"

"Yeah," I said. "And the other vampire."

Patrick cleared his throat. "We found the remains of . . . er, Melvin. And the ashes of the Wraith."

Wraith? Tainted vampire? My mind was starting to spin. I didn't know what these terms meant. I wasn't sure I cared.

"Ah. Ralph tried to save me first." I said it just in case he got points or a gold star or something. She was the queen. Maybe she could knight him and bequeath him some land or serfs or whatever.

"Ralph's a gentleman, sure enough," said Patsy. "Melvin's attached himself to you, hon. He likes you."

I looked to my right. I didn't see anything. Anyone. All the same, chills raced up my spine. "When you say attached . . . you mean his ghost is following me around?"

"I know it's hard to believe," said Patsy kindly, "but it's true."

"Oh, I believe it." I had validation for all those years of searching and theorizing and traipsing through godforsaken places. Hysteria threatened, but I managed to hold it at bay. "Mom's gonna love this place. Oh, and Dad. He's really wanted to use that new spectrometer."

"I'm afraid I can't let you invite them to town," said Patsy.

Panic erupted. They didn't know my parents were in Broken Heart. I had no idea if Mom and Dad had been unavailable because the phones crapped out or because they'd run into trouble. But if I was sitting in the living room with the queen, then who—or what—had gotten hold of my parents?

Wait. Calm down, Libby. I didn't have any facts. I needed to quit operating on emotion. These seemed like nice . . . er, people, so they'd probably question me and let me go. Then I could try contacting my parents again.

It was next to impossible to keep my mind on track because Ralph kept jumping into my thoughts. Would it be too junior-high to ask if he'd said anything about me? Yeah. It would. I wondered if I'd see him again.

As if on cue, Ralph walked into the living room. The fire's song melded into a low, sweet crooning. I leapt from the couch, unaccountably happy to see him.

"Ralph!" I hurried across the room and threw myself into his arms. "You're okay! You're really okay!"

"So are you," he murmured, pulling back to look me over. His hand curved on my cheek. My heart tripled its beat. Heat poured through me. His aura was golden, pure as sunshine. I wanted to bask in it. He smelled like orange spice, a cinnamon-smoky scent, both sweet and tart.

I leaned forward and blew on the spot under his left ear. He sucked in a breath and I felt his lips brush my earlobe.

"Do y'all need a room?" asked Patsy drolly. "Or can we get down to business?"

Her voice shattered the spell. We both blinked at each other and broke apart.

"What just happened?" I whispered.

"I don't know," he answered. "But I hope it happens again."

"You two sit down," snapped Patsy.

I turned around, my fingers intertwining with Ralph's. Everyone looked at us in astonishment.

"What?" I asked.

"This isn't high school and you ain't behind the bleachers."

Patsy sounded very irritated. We both sat on the couch like two children sent to the principal's office, but I kept my grip on his hand. My gaze was drawn to Ralph. He looked so delicious. I wanted to sit on his lap and lick him.

"I don't know what's going on here," said Patsy. "But it's weird."

It didn't feel weird. It felt right. I couldn't keep from staring at Ralph. I was intoxicated by his nearness. I thirsted for him. "You are so fine."

"What?" Patsy asked, her voice suspicious.

I coughed. "Wine. I asked if I could have some wine."

"We have enough stupidity around here. I don't keep booze in the house. Ralph, go make her some tea. Take your time."

"Aw," I whined. I didn't want Ralph to leave. Not ever. My attraction for him was otherworldly. The dragon had kissed me. Now I had a kinship with fire, with passion.

Ralph didn't seem to want to leave, either, but he obviously couldn't disobey his queen. He took my hand and kissed it, then went off to do Patsy's bidding.

I looked morosely at Patsy. Then my gaze dropped to her belly.

"You're the queen of the vampires, right?" I frowned. "How can you be pregnant? Aren't you dead?"

"It's complicated. I'm sorta queen of the lycanthropes, too," said Patsy. Her expression looked as if she'd swallowed glass. Guess there was some tension there. I couldn't imagine trying to rule vampires and werewolves. I hadn't mastered balancing my checkbook, so keeping the balance between two traditional enemies was beyond my skills. Then it hit me. Oh, crap. I pointed at Patsy's belly. "*Loup de sang*. You're *loup de sang*."

"How did you know that?" The question came from Gabriel and his tone wasn't friendly.

"We live, breathe, eat, and drink the paranormal. Mom's written several books. Vampires. Werewolves. Ghosts. Can you believe she actually uncovered a diary from a French fur trader who . . . " I trailed off. My whole body went cold. "Did you say your name was Gabriel? Gabriel *Marchand*? Saint Thomas on toast . . . you're the first blood wolf in history."

"Wow. She's good," said Patsy. "Look, she seems harmless, so I say we let her go."

Patrick shook his head. "I don't think that's wise."

"Well, you're not the queen, are you?" she asked. She looked at me, her blue eyes suddenly intense, mesmerizing. "You will leave Broken Heart. You will forget everything you've seen. You will return to tell PRIS there's nothing here."

Her voice seduced, beckoned, promised. I recognized that sexy do-what-I-want undertone.

She stared at me, and I stared at her. Finally, I

said, "Is this the part where I call you mistress and agree to bring you victims?"

Patsy looked shocked. She stood up, crossed to the couch, and took my hands in hers. Once again, I was drawn into her forceful gaze.

"Forget everything you've seen and heard in Broken Heart. Forget Broken Heart. Tell PRIS nothing is here."

I said nothing, hoping they might believe her second attempt worked. Maybe they would take me back to our car and leave me alone. I still needed to find out what had happened to Mom and Dad. Even though Broken Heart was filled with the evidence we needed to prove the paranormal world was real, it was too dangerous. I was more than happy to forget about this town and what lived here.

"It didn't work," said Gabriel. "Did it? Ralph said it wouldn't."

His voice held soft menace. I swallowed the knot suddenly lodged in my throat. He was the most dangerous one in the room. I didn't want to cross him. He rose from the divan and stepped toward me. Patrick had shifted as well, his gaze on mine. Patsy wasn't moving, either. I slipped my hands from hers.

The singing changed harmonies. It rose in alarm, a chorus of warning.

I stood up, unsure about what I could do against

people who were faster, stronger, and smarter than I was. I didn't care who they were; they couldn't hold me against my will. I slid closer to the fireplace; the heat beckoned me. I craved more of its warmth.

"I'd ask nicely, but I can't give you a choice," said Patsy. I heard real regret in her voice. "You might as well get used to the idea, Libby. You're not leaving Broken Heart."

Chapter 7

"I won't breathe a word," I promised, my heart thundering. "I'll never return. I swear!"

"I believe you," said Patsy. "But it doesn't much matter. You know too much about Broken Heart that we can't make you forget."

I couldn't form a response. I had no doubts Patsy and her friends would keep me here. Fear skittered through me. I hated not feeling in control.

"You can't hold me hostage," I said. Anger pulsed low and heavy. The fire blazing so close to me just added to the heat filling my body. "People will notice I'm gone."

"Will they?" asked Patrick.

I realized then that, even though their glamour didn't work on me, I got the impression that they'd had lots of success with others. Would PRIS forget me? My parents?

The ball of anger refused to dissipate. The ugly emotion threatened to consume me.

I glared at Patsy. "I'm not one of your subjects! You can't tell me what to do!"

Patsy's gaze hardened. "What are you, twelve? Put on your big-girl panties and deal with it."

Rage surged through me. I grappled with its ferocity, trying to get it under control. Clenching my fists, I stared at the floor, listening to the fire's swelling music.

I hadn't lost my temper in a long, long time. I was furious. At myself. At the circumstances. At everything.

"Do you see that?" asked Patsy.

"Yes," said Gabriel. "What is it?"

"Jay-sus," muttered Patrick.

Heat pulsed in my every nerve ending. I felt as though the very air around me was spinning. I felt hot. The whirling air felt hot, too.

Gabriel grabbed his wife by the shoulders and tucked her behind him. Patrick went to stand next to his friends. They all stared at me.

"You can't make me stay here," I said. My voice sounded odd. Deep and raspy. Even my words felt like they were on fire.

"Demon possession," suggested Patsy.

"No. Something else," said Gabriel. "She's mortal. I've never seen anything like this."

"Gabriel, I think it's wise to get Patsy out of here."

"Are you kidding?" asked Patsy. "I'll blast her or something."

"Don't argue, sweetheart," said Gabriel. "Think of our babies."

I heard their conversation, but I no longer cared what they said, what they thought, what they did.

I watched Gabriel and Patsy retreat. My vision was dark around the edges, as if I were viewing the world through binoculars. The music rose, triumphant.

"Libby," said Patrick, his voice low and calm. "We didn't mean to upset you."

What a liar. Electric heat crackled along my limbs. My fury was a powerful thing, nearly alive. I had no control . . . whatever-this-was controlled me. It was almost as if I floated outside myself, watching some scary woman wield a terrible ability.

The air twisting around me picked up books from the end tables, tossed lamps to the floor. The coffee table exploded. Shards flew everywhere. Mangled wood joined the debris zipping around me. The couch detonated. Batting filled the air like snow.

I looked down, dispassionate, and saw flames licking my skin. I knew I should be afraid, but I wasn't. This was part of me. Part of who I was now. The fire told me the truth, and I embraced it.

I couldn't see Patrick. He'd probably left, too.

The next burst of energy hit the hearth. Stone shattered. White dust plumed. The fireplace cracked in half and fell inward, dousing the cozy fire. I felt my power wobble.

"Libby!"

Ralph's voice cut through the roaring symphony in my head. I turned toward the doorway. He stood there, the cup of tea in his hand falling to the floor.

He walked into the maelstrom, his anxious gaze on mine. Loose book pages flapped at him. Debris pummeled him. He didn't stop. He didn't look away.

The minute his hands clamped onto my shoulders, I felt my quaking power drain. I collapsed, or would have. Ralph scooped me up and held me close. I felt his lips press against my forehead.

"It's okay," he murmured. "It's okay."

I don't know how long he stood there holding me. Long enough for the dust to clear. Long enough for me to see the damage I'd done. Long enough to realize that Patrick hadn't made it out of the room.

"Oh my God." I scrambled out of Ralph's embrace. He was so surprised at my sudden, frantic movements that he let go. I fell to the ground and immediately crawled to Patrick, lying so still on the floor. My insides quivered coldly.

Wood and stone shards were embedded in his body. Most of the projectiles were small, all except the one piercing his heart. The fragment sticking out of his chest was large, probably what was left of a coffee table leg. Blood spattered his clothes. His eyes were closed and he was so limp. Dead. *Really* dead.

"I killed him." I started plucking out all the pieces. I was no longer worried about leaving Broken Heart. I was worried about leaving the earthly plane. No one I'd met so far struck me as the forgiving types.

"Libby." Ralph crouched beside me and covered my shaking hands with his. "It's not like in the movies. A stake to the heart doesn't kill the undead."

"Are you sure?"

"I told you. The only way to kill us is to remove our heads. Or get us into very bright light." Ralph's gaze was kind. And he wasn't freaking out, so I had to believe that Patrick would be okay. "Stay here, Libby. I'll get help."

I nodded. I looked at Patrick. I didn't know him. Hell, I didn't even like him. I hadn't meant to do this.

Yeah, I could try to run. But even if I managed to escape the vampires tonight, it didn't mean I'd escape them forever. They had pushed me and, in a way, they'd unleashed whatever scary thing had happened. But I couldn't go. I needed to fix my mistake. I figured there was one sure way to help a dying vampire.

I grabbed the stake I'd unintentionally jabbed

into Patrick's heart and yanked it out. Blood burbled out of the jagged hole. *Oh, God.* I took off my sweater and pushed it against the wound.

Finding a sharp object was easy enough. I grabbed a sliver of stone and slashed my wrist. It stung like hell, but I'm sure it hurt a lot less than getting stabbed in the heart.

I held my bloodied flesh against Patrick's mouth. Seconds passed and nothing happened. When Patrick's lips finally moved against the offering, I yelped. His fangs dug into my wrist; the pain was excruciating.

He drank and drank. After a while, I felt lightheaded and dizzy. My vision grayed. My hand slipped away from the sweater I'd been pressing against his injury. The material fell off and I could see that the hole was gone. Relief flooded me. He would be okay.

His eyes popped open, those silvery orbs filled with accusation. He freed my arm and sat up, then rubbed his mouth, as if to get the taste of me off his lips.

I didn't blame him. Not after what I'd done.

"I'm sorry," I said.

I scooted away from him, feeling dizzy and strange. Closing my eyes made my head spin worse, so I stared at the floor. Loud voices, scurrying feet, banging and cursing and scraping infiltrated my mind. Somewhere in the noise, I heard

Ralph's voice. "Damn it, Patrick. What did you do to her?"

"What did I do to *her*?" he yelled. "She damned near killed me!"

"Looks like she saved you, too. What's wrong with her wrist? It's still bleeding," Ralph asked, ignoring Patrick's ire. "Your saliva didn't heal her. Hey! Why is her sweater off? She's only in her bra!"

"Who are you? Her mother?" This voice was Patsy's. "Did she give you blood, Patrick?"

"Of course she did, otherwise I wouldn't be talking. Her blood is strange. It tastes metallic." I heard the grimace in his tone. "She's got a helluva temper."

"We pushed her too far," said Gabriel. "None of us would accept being a prisoner so easily."

Huh. I hadn't expected understanding from Mr. Grumpy. I looked up and tried to focus. No good. I couldn't figure out how many people were in the room. I felt hands on my shoulders. Ralph.

Suddenly, I felt better. It was like energy flowed into me, healing what was injured. I looked at him. He was removing his shirt. Wow. He had nice abs. Crisp brown curls feathered his chest and arrowed down to his jeans. He helped me put on the shirt and then buttoned it for me.

"What the hell happened in that cemetery?" Patsy's blue eyes studied me and then Ralph.

Patrick said, "It seems Ralph was set on fire."

"So was Libby," said Ralph. His eyes were on

mine. He nibbled his bottom lip, distracting me from the conversation. "The dragon took human form and kissed her. They were both on fire, but neither one burned."

"I'm burning now," I said. I waved my hand in front of my face and smiled seductively. "I'm really hot."

"Me, too," said Ralph. He scooted closer to me. His scent was stronger and so was his aura. It shined brilliantly.

"What do you think this all means?" asked Patrick.

I didn't think he was asking me. And I was right.

"Whatever's going on, it seems to be connected to Ralph, too." This was Gabriel's observation.

"We need to rouse Stan," said Patsy. "C'mon. We need to get you both down to the lab."

"The lab?" I heard concern edge Ralph's voice. "What for?"

"Don't make me play the queen card, damn it. I'm tired, I'm hungry, and I'm hormonal."

Ralph picked me up, and I closed my eyes.

"Welcome to Broken Heart," said Patrick. "Looks like you're walking evidence of the paranormal."

I glared down at him, not quite brave enough to tell him to shut up.

I don't remember passing out, but I do remember waking up. I was lying on an examination table. I scrambled off so fast I ripped the waxy paper covering it.

Ralph sat in a chair next to the table, watching me. "You're safe."

"Yeah, right." I walked to the door and yanked on the handle. Locked. I turned around and glared at him. "What's going on?"

"The doctor is going to run some tests."

"Why?"

"Because we need to figure out why you went all Firestarter out there."

"You're not exactly fire-free, buddy." I rubbed my arms. I was cold. I didn't like it. I also didn't like the silence. There was no singing in here. No warmth.

"It feels like they turned on the air-conditioning."

"They did. Dragons don't like the cold, and if your new self is related to what the dragon did to you . . . " He trailed off, avoiding my gaze.

It seemed the air-conditioning had also managed to chill the odd attraction between us. Although he was still number one on my yummy-man list, I was grateful I didn't have the uncontrollable urge to jump his bones.

"Just relax," said Ralph. "I'm in here, too. We can be lab rats together."

"Oh, hell no." Once again, I turned to the door and pounded on it. "Let me out! Let me out *now*!"

"Libby."

My name held soft reproach. I leaned my forehead against the white metal door. "I don't want to be a lab rat. What's this doctor's name? Franken-stein?"

I hated white, sterile rooms like this one. Other than the chair Ralph occupied, there was no other place to plant my butt. I returned to the table and sat on its edge.

"Dr. Michaels is nice, and he's very smart. As a bonus, he's also human."

"We'll see about that," I said. I couldn't pinpoint any particular reason why I didn't like physicians or hospitals. I always got the creepy-crawlies. And I had them bad right now.

The door opened. A man entered. I had a nice view of his balding head since he was looking at a clipboard. He was short and paunchy and, overall, he reminded me of a sad-eyed beagle.

Then he lifted his head, his smile reassuring.

I didn't think anything else could shock me.

I was wrong.

I nearly fell off the table. "Uncle Archie! I thought you were dead!"

Chapter 8

"Seraphina!" Archie's expression was a cross between happy and horrified. I felt the same way. I was thrilled he was still breathing and pissed off he hadn't bothered to let me know. Or my parents. Or any of his coworkers at PRIS.

"Wait," said Ralph. He looked at Archie. "You're not Stan?" His gaze slanted to me. "And you're not Libby?"

"My first name is Archibald," said Archie. "I switched to my middle name when I started working for the Consortium."

"I've always hated my first name. I go by Libby now." I glanced at Ralph. His expression was thoughtful. I realized I was still wearing his shirt. Someone must've loaned him one. Too bad. Viewing him without a shirt was like indulging in an all-day truffle. But I was not here to lust after Ralph. That was just a perk.

I had bigger worries right now. The man who'd been like family to me had abandoned us. Why?

Almost ten years ago, when I was thirteen, we followed an anonymous tip to an isolated farm deep in the South Carolina woods. We'd been told "nightwalkers" inhabited the dilapidated building and that outsiders who ventured onto the property were attacked by savage wolves. Come to think of it, that whole situation reminded me of Broken Heart's setup.

My mother and I did a perimeter check at the tree line. Perimeter checks were how my parents kept me away from the action. Anyway, Archie took his equipment around the barn and Dad went to the crumbling house.

The barn exploded. All we found of Archie were his glasses, one scorched shoe, and a melted EMF detector.

"What happened?" I asked. "We thought you died in the explosion."

"A vampire saved my life."

"No, *really*?" Hel-*lo*. I'd figured out he'd hooked up with the undead. I got it. Vampires were real. But I hadn't quite grasped that Archie had left behind his life on purpose. "Mom cried for weeks. She thought it was her fault."

"I'm sorry about that. I really am. Your mother

is . . . well, your mother. I was tired of PRIS, Sera."
He shook his head. "Libby. Patrick O'Halloran
pulled me out of the blaze."

I gaped at him. "You mean poof boy?"

Archie blinked.

"Yes," said Ralph, chuckling. "That's Patrick."

We both turned to Archie, waiting for his explanation.

"He offered me unlimited funds to carry out real
research." Archie stared at his clipboard, his cheeks
mottling. "Making a clean break was one of the conditions of my agreement with the Consortium. I regret I was unable to say proper good-byes, but you
know how Dora is." He made wriggling motions
with his fingers. "She's got that thing she does with
her eyes. I never could lie to her."

"Yeah. Me, neither."

We contemplated each other in silence.

"Trust me, Libby. I know you're here under
duress, but you won't come to harm. Now, tell me
what happened," he said in his serious-doctor tone.

I shrugged. "Beats me. The Mod Squad was closing in around me, I got really upset, and everything
went nuclear. Things started exploding." I hesitated. "And I think I can hear fire singing."

Ralph nodded. "I . . . uh, think I can hear that,
too."

"Really?" I turned to him, feeling so relieved. If I
was nuts, he was, too. Was that a good thing?

"That tops the weird-o-meter," said Archie, shaking his head.

Ouch. In a town full of weird, being told I was the weirdest wasn't comforting. "So, it had something to do with the dragon kissing me?"

I explained the woman in the cemetery, how she'd grabbed me, kissed me, and set me on fire. And then I'd set Ralph on fire. And ta-da . . . I can hear flame musicals.

"I'd like to try something," said Archie. "Both of you turn around."

Ralph and I shared a look. We stood up and turned around. I was uncomfortable. What was Archie up to?

I heard the rustling of cloth and then a scritching sound.

"What do you hear?" asked Archie.

"I'll take 'what is the sound of silence' for three hundred, Alex," I said.

Ralph laughed.

"Seriously," said Archie, sounding annoyed. "What do you hear?"

"You. Babbling."

He sighed. Then I heard another scritching noise. A dulcet tone shimmied through me. I glanced at Ralph. He was already looking at me, his eyes dark. He took my hand and we turned, our gazes drawn to the lighter in Archie's hand. The flame was small, but its song was not. It was pure, cleansing, just like the fire.

"What are you two doing?"

I barely heard Archie's question. I reached for the lighter, but he pulled away. The fire went out.

"No!" Ralph pushed Archie against the door and I yanked the little plastic Bic out of his fingers. I flicked it on and the flame sprang to life, singing, singing.

Ralph dropped Archie, who landed with a thud. Then he joined me and, together, we listened to the song. For the first time, I heard words.

I looked at Ralph. "Is that . . . Def Leppard?"

"Yeah. It's 'Rock of Ages.'" He dipped his finger into the flame and it slid along his skin. When it hit his shirt, the material burned away. The flame danced on his wrist. So seductive. I leaned down and licked it.

The fire invaded my mouth. Ambrosia. I embraced Ralph. His eyes pinned mine. He was burning. So was I. The flames feasted on his shirt, not on his skin. He was a vampire whose fire danced and loved, but didn't char or destroy. It loved me, too.

His arms surrounded me, and so did his flames. We burned together. I sucked in the fire and it raced down my throat. I felt the soot coat my tongue.

"L-Libby?"

I looked down at Archie, barely registering his

look of terror. Then I saw the smoke curling out of my nostrils.

What the hell?

The door burst open and someone dressed in a silver hazmat suit pointed an extinguisher at me. White foam exploded from the nozzle and blanketed us.

The music was instantly silenced. "No!" I cried.

Archie and the fireman backed out. I didn't understand the look on Archie's face. Like he didn't know me.

The door shut and we heard the lock snick.

Ralph and I looked at each other.

"That was weird." He stepped back, wiping off his face and shaking the foam off his hands. Then he scrubbed at his hair.

"Yeah." I flipped the wheel on the Bic. *Flick. Flick.* "It won't work." Panic wormed through me. I thrust the lighter at Ralph. "Fix this."

"No, Libby." He held up his hands. "I don't want the fire. It's . . . wrong."

"Wrong? How could it be wrong?" Was he insane? I needed the flame. We needed it. "Please, Ralph." I was desperate to have fire again. I knew I was acting a little crazed, but I couldn't stop myself. Fire was life. Desperation made me flick the wheel over and over, but it never sparked.

"Libby. Stop." He plucked the useless lighter

from my hand. I reached for it and he pushed my hand away. "Damn it! Enough, already."

I sucked in a breath. I was shaking. And cold. Had they kicked up the air-conditioning again? "What's wrong with me?" I whispered. "Why do I need it so much? And why can you resist?"

"Two reasons," he said. "Michael and Stephen."

I stared at him. "I don't understand."

"My sons," he said. "What I feel now . . . what I feel for you, it can't be more important than my sons. They're only three, and they need me. I need them. You . . . me . . . this fire thing . . ." He shook his head. "I can't do this. Feel this way. No more fire."

No more us. My heart dropped to my toes. He thought our attraction was just about the flame. The dragon magic. The implication still hurt.

He tucked the lighter into his pocket. We were covered in puffs of white. I wiped off my face and arms. I tried to rein in my emotions, but they were a tornado.

The door opened and Archie poked his head in. "Ralph, come on."

"Wait a minute," I said. "What about me?"

"I'll be back for you," said Archie.

I looked at Ralph. He stepped toward me, hand stretching as if to take mine, and then he hesitated. He dropped his arm. "Everything's going to be okay, Libby."

He turned and slipped through the door. After it was shut, I heard the lock engage.

I was a prisoner. No fire. No Ralph. No hope.

My eyes opened. What the hell?

The last thing I remembered was Ralph leaving the examination room.

I was lying on a somewhat comfortable bed in a small, white room. These people really had a thing about white.

I'd been dressed in a pair of pink silk pajamas that were way too big. Patsy. She was at least half a foot taller than me and pregnant. Good thing the pants had a string tie.

My bare feet touched the floor, but it wasn't cold. It wasn't tile, either. I scrunched my toes against the slick surface. I'd never felt anything like it before.

My head felt fuzzy, but I didn't need all my faculties to know I was in a prison. Well, what did I expect? One of the royal suites?

I stood up and looked around.

Behind me was a small door. I pushed a silver button next to it, and the door slid open. The bathroom was tiny. A stand-up shower, toilet, and sink with mirror. One shelf on the opposite wall with towels, wash cloths, and a small assortment of soaps and shampoos.

I used the facilities, then wandered back into the other room. Other than the bed there wasn't any furniture. No TV or magazines, either. I looked at the ceiling. I couldn't detect any video cameras, but I knew I was being monitored. I knew Archie . . . no, Stan, had probably built this facility.

He was brilliant. Stan wasn't just a gifted scientist; he also held degrees in medicine and engineering. He understood things about the world most people never would.

An intense paranormal experience had drawn him into PRIS, and soon he left his highbrow research job at a pharmaceutical company to work full-time with my parents. I was three or four years old when he joined us, so I'd grown up with him. Stan wasn't the kind of person you could get close to. He was too analytical. He picked apart everything, which made him a great scientist and a lousy conversationalist. The man had no social skills.

Still, when he died, I'd cried for weeks. He'd been part of our family. I didn't know how to feel about his betrayal. I couldn't decide if I was mad or sad about him walking away from us so easily.

And he joined up with the very creatures we'd tried to find. My whole life my parents had researched the paranormal. Oh, they got lucky every now and then, but mostly they got nada. Their enthusiasm and persistence never waned. My mother didn't know the meaning of rejection. She didn't care that other people laughed at her and PRIS. Usually when she and Dad were invited as "experts" on talk shows, it was only to make them look like crackpots.

I sat on the bed and let my feet swing back and forth. My wrist still ached where I'd slit it to feed Patrick. I remembered Ralph had said vampire saliva had an enzyme that healed feeding wounds very quickly. He was puzzled about why mine hadn't healed.

I sighed. Were my parents looking for me? Were they okay? I had to believe the best, because the worst was unthinkable. You've never met two people who so believed in things that couldn't be proven. My mother had *faith*. The kind of faith that was unshakable. And my father believed in her—even when she claimed to be kidnapped by aliens and used for experimentation. You could never accuse my mother of being boring.

Once again I stood up, then I walked to the clear door of my cell. I tapped my fingernails against the plastic. It was at least a foot thick. The cell across from mine was empty. The hallway was dimly lit and I couldn't see down to either end. I heard nothing.

I turned around and assessed the space. There was enough room to do yoga. I didn't know how long I would be kept here. I didn't think the queen would let me go. Unless they figured out a way to make me permanently forget everything I'd seen. Or killed me.

Fear uncoiled and slithered through me. I didn't know what would happen next. I couldn't be sure they wouldn't just kill me. Ten years ago I would've said Stan would never have allowed such a thing. But I didn't know him anymore.

I wanted to think Ralph would prevent them from doing anything too drastic. He was one of them, though. And he hadn't stopped them from putting me in this prison. I couldn't stop the little bump-de-bump my heart did when I thought about Ralph. But he didn't feel that way about me, obviously.

What was with the fire? What was with the dragon? How had the dying woman changed me? And how had I changed Ralph?

He was a father.

I couldn't wrap my brain about that fact. He was damned sexy for a daddy. Not to mention he was undead. How did a vampire raise mortal children? How did a vampire even have kids?

For all our studies of these creatures, we had to rely heavily on mythology, folklore, and eyewitness accounts. It had never occurred to me that vampires might have the same hopes and worries as humans.

And Ralph didn't want me. He thought the fire bound us, and maybe he was right. But I wanted him anyway.

I'd never really had a boyfriend. I'd never settled anywhere long enough to meet men, much less date them. Only one had stuck around long enough to meet my parents—on the slim chance he might actually make it into my pants—and that had been the end of the relationship. Hey, love me, love my parents. So far, no man I'd managed to date had been able to do either one.

Honestly, Ralph was the first guy to whom I felt va-va-voom attracted. Most of the time, I knew I was *supposed* to feel a certain way. I could look at Brad Pitt and think, "He's cute and, hey, nice abs." But that heart-pounding, knee-shaking, palm-sweating attraction between two people had never been mine to experience . . . until Ralph scooped me into his arms and kept me safe from the wolves.

Oh, what did it matter? Talk about being from two different worlds. Sheesh. I shut out the rest of my worries. I couldn't do anything until they let me out. I needed a clear mind and to restore my sense of calm. The clothes were too big for me to do a yoga routine, so I shucked them. Luckily, I still had on my underwear, but no bra. Oh, well. My parents and I once lived in a nudist colony, where the phrase "let it all hang out" was taken literally. I was very comfortable with my body. Nudity was nothing to be ashamed of, and I wasn't.

I shucked off the pajamas and put them on the bed. Then I put my palms together and stood in Mountain pose. *Breathe in. Breathe out.* I decided to do Sun Salutation.

I focused on the poses and pushed away mental distractions. I did Cobra pose: I stretched out on my stomach, then put my palms flat on the floor, lifted my torso off the ground, and bent back, my eyes raised to the ceiling.

After a few seconds, I realized someone was watching me. I released the position and rolled to my knees, crossing my arms over my breasts.

Through the clear door of the cell, Ralph pried his baby blues off my chest and grinned sheepishly. "Uh . . . hi, Libby."

Chapter 9

"Please turn around so I can get dressed." Being comfortable with my naked body was one thing; showing off my assets to Ralph was something else. I was angry. He'd left me. He had fire issues, too, but they were letting him walk around free.

He dutifully turned around. I put on the pajamas and then strode to the metal door.

"Okay, I'm decent."

"The adjective I'd use is spectacular." Ralph turned around, his cheeks flushed.

"Are you blushing?" I asked. "Can vampires do that?"

"No. And no." He cleared his throat and held up a white paper bag. "I thought you might be hungry," he said, talking a bit louder so I could hear him through the door.

"Aw, that's so nice of you," I said in a saccharine voice with a similarly raised voice. My sarcasm was ruined by my growling stomach.

"I brought you a hamburger with the works, large order of fries, and a chocolate shake. It's my specialty." His smile dimmed. "I'm a short-order cook at the Old Sass Café."

"Too bad you're not a prison guard. With a key."

He flinched. "This is just until we figure out what's going on, Libby." He placed his hand on the plastic window. "It's for your safety. And ours."

"Because you already have fire power, right? Or did you avoid a cell just because you're one of them?"

"I've been taught how to control my fire. You'll learn how, too."

"In here?"

He had the grace to look uncomfortable, maybe even ashamed. "I'm sorry." His gaze flicked to mine, and I saw the fire dancing in the blue orbs. He really did look sorry, and I felt an answering fire inside me. We were part of the same magic, the same passion. I felt it even with the barrier of the door between us.

I wondered if Ralph did, too.

Desperation flailed my pride. I pressed my palm against his, although the plastic prevented us from touching. "Please, Ralph. Let me out. I'll leave. I'll . . . never come back."

He looked at me, and I thought he might say something, something that would bridge the gap between us. That would reassure me.

"Libby . . ."

"Yes?"

He shook his head, but couldn't quite pry his gaze from mine. The fire was inside him, calling to me. I heard its song.

"You hear it, don't you?" I whispered.

"Yes," he admitted. "I crave it, too. More than you could ever know."

Oh, I knew. The difference between us was he could push it away, probably even lock it up. I didn't have the strength to deny the flame. It wanted Ralph. I wanted Ralph. It was like my heart couldn't beat without his.

Finally, he broke eye contact. He pointed to the right side of my cell. "They'll give you the food through a slot in that wall."

"Ralph." Censure vibrated.

"Please, Libby. Just . . . don't."

Disappointment weighed heavily on me. I guess I should give the guy a break, but I had hoped he would rescue me. I was getting used to it, after all. Ralph, my undead knight in shining armor.

I sighed. "I'm a vegan."

His eyebrows rose. "So . . . hamburgers aren't your thing."

"I don't eat animals or wear their flesh. Anything made from animal by-products is out, too."

"By-products?"

"Milk, eggs, cheese . . . you know, by-products."

"Ah. Chocolate milk shakes are out, too." He nodded. "Got it. I'll figure out something vegan-ish for tomorrow night's dinner."

"Thanks."

An awkward silence fell. He seemed reluctant to leave. Why? He'd made clear his intentions. Maybe he couldn't quite resist the fire, either. Dragonfire was not the same as his vampire power. Oh, what did I know? Fire was probably fire. And I was still a prisoner.

"They might let me out of this place, but I'll still be a prisoner. Won't I?"

I waited for him to deny it.

His gaze captured mine and I saw his regret. "I know this isn't fair. I'm sorry. I really am."

Hurt settled like a cold lump in my stomach. "And that's supposed to make me feel better?"

"My sons lost their mother and they nearly lost me, too. Being a vampire isn't something I chose, but it's better than being six feet under." He blew out a breath. "You're not the only one dealing with new changes, Libby. You're not the only one with something to lose."

I strained my neck to watch him walk to the end of the hallway. He was swallowed by darkness. I heard the faint clang of a metal door as it opened and closed.

Then I was alone.

"Patient Monroe, please enjoy your dinner." A mechanical voice startled me. I looked up, which was kinda stupid, especially since the voice didn't emanate from the ceiling. I couldn't determine its source.

A square door opened about two feet above my bed. The bag sat on a metal tray that slid out. My parents were vegan, too, and had raised me in the lifestyle. I had veered from veganism only once, and eating the steak made me so ill I vomited. I couldn't stand the smell of leather, either. We won't talk about my views on milk. Yuck.

I removed the bag and took out the fries, which were still crispy and hot. I returned the bag, but not before I peeked into the little doorway. Shoot. It was closed on the other side.

Usually the smell of cooked meat made my stomach lurch, but for some reason the hamburger made me salivate. Ew. No. Still, I unwrapped it and inhaled the scent. Oh, man. I was tempted to take a bite.

What was happening to me? I was in love with fire. And now I craved meat. I threw the hamburger back into the bag. I ignored the chocolate shake.

"Hey, Mr. Roboto! You got any water?" I munched on the fries.

"Please enjoy the water available in your personal bathroom."

"Gee, thanks. Do I have to use my hands or can you give me a cup?"

"Cups are available in the convenient dispenser next to your sink."

What dispenser? I got off the bed and went into the bathroom. I hadn't noticed it before, but there was a little silver dispenser with tiny paper cups. I filled one up and drank the water. Then I refilled the cup and carried it with me to the bed.

I used to think my weird life couldn't get any weirder.

Was I wrong, or what?

I'm not sure what woke me up. I lay on the bed, my eyes still closed. My muscles ached from the cramped sleeping quarters. I turned on my side and let my mind drift.

Once I'd finished the fries and put my trash on the tray, it zipped back into the wall. I tried to make conversation with Mr. Roboto, but he only offered instructions related to my cell. I figured out that I could control the lights simply by voice commands. Finally, I got so bored I turned off the light and went to sleep.

"Libby."

Stan's voice sounded strained and raspy. I opened my eyes. The lights were on full and the brightness stabbed my eyeballs. Ugh. I covered my face and said, "Lights fifty percent."

They dimmed and I stumbled off the bed and toward the cell door. Stan looked pale. Sweat poured off his face and the fringe of hair surrounding his bald spot stuck straight up. His white lab coat was wrinkled and stained.

"You look like hell. How long have I been out?" I asked. Hope surged. "Are you letting me go?"

"You've only been asleep a couple of hours." He studied me, frowning. "I'm afraid we can't release you."

I didn't like how he was looking at me. I stepped back and hugged myself. Foreboding swirled in my belly. "What's going on?"

"Just tell me what you did to Patrick."

My heart skipped a beat. "I already said I was sorry! I didn't mean to stake him. And he was fine. Just ask Ralph."

"Did you give anything to him?"

"Other than my blood?"

"Yes," he hissed. His gaze cut down the hallway and then he looked back at me. "Please, Libby! Did you jab him with something? Did you slip him a pill or . . . or a tincture?"

"A *tincture*? C'mon! I'm not a spy," I said, annoyed with his questions. "I slit my wrist and let him drink my blood."

"Maybe you coming to Broken Heart isn't a coincidence, after all." His expression turned cold. "You have an unusual background. They found me. They could've found you, too."

"Who?"

"Vampires. Only the Wraiths or Hu Mua Lan got to you." He scowled and stepped back, shaking his head. "I don't think you're Lia's minion. I mean, not on purpose."

"What are you talking about?" I asked. Dread squeezed my stomach. "I don't know anyone named Hu whoever. I don't know what a Wraith is. And I didn't do anything to Patrick."

"Yes, you did," he said in a shaking voice. His gaze pinned mine. "You poisoned him."

Chapter 10

The shock of Stan's accusation nearly buckled my knees. I grabbed for the wall and sucked in a steadying breath. Oh my God. Did they think I tried to kill someone?

I couldn't even speak. I stared at Stan, and he looked down at the floor, his face going scarlet. I knew then he didn't believe I'd done anything wrong. But he was beholden to these vampires. I knew his loyalty belonged to them.

The faint clang of the hallway door opening and closing had my heart thumping in earnest. Fear was a live thing squirming inside me as I listened to booted feet thudding toward us. The jailers had come to tell me my appeal had been denied. Hah. Stan glanced at me, sympathy in his hound-dog gaze.

Patrick's twin, Lorcan, arrived. I assumed it was Lorcan because, while he looked pissed off, he didn't look poisoned. Plus, his outline was purple. Patrick's was blue.

A tall man with muscles on his muscles took position on the left side of Stan. He was dressed in black leather pants and matching vest. Ugh. Animal flesh. His feet were encased in black biker boots with silver buckles. He had jade green eyes and the face of a *GQ* model. His long black hair was pulled into a ponytail. Hostile didn't begin to describe his attitude toward me. He was outlined in red.

"Did she tell you what she did?" he asked. His accent was German. He looked like he could break me in half. Worse, he looked like he *wanted* to. I shuddered.

Stan shook his head. "Whatever she did, I don't believe she did it on purpose."

"We'll see about that." Lorcan's voice was thick with Irish. "If her poison kills me brother, then darlin' Jessica dies, too."

"Jessica?" I vaguely remembered the name, but couldn't connect it to anyone I'd met so far. I backed away, but there was nowhere to go. If they opened that door, they could easily capture and subdue me. "I didn't even touch her!"

"Jessica is Patrick's wife," said Stan. "They're bound. Bound vampires are connected body, mind, and soul. If Patrick dies . . . so does she."

"I tried to help him! I swear the only thing I gave Patrick was my blood." My gaze collided with Stan's as we both reached the same conclusion. "Do you think my blood poisoned him?"

He frowned. "I don't see how . . . unless you ingested something on purpose. Something that wouldn't hurt you."

"Use your big brain, Stan! What could I take that would hurt the freaking undead, but leave me alive? Aren't vampires indestructible?"

"We can be killed," said Lorcan.

"By sunlight and . . . and beheading. That's what Ralph told me." My mind raced, trying to piece together information I'd learned inadvertently. There was something else that could kill vampires, too. "Patsy said Tainted vampires were sick. Do they get the Taint from humans?" My eyes went wide. "Do . . . do I have that? Oh my God! Stan, do I have the Taint?"

"No. Humans can't get the Taint. And that's not what is harming Patrick."

The big guy with the green eyes and the assassin smile looked me over. "We may have jumped to conclusions. How quickly can you test her blood?"

Stanley shrugged. "I should be able to test it against known substances fairly quickly."

"This has something to do with the dragon," I muttered. "She changed me, didn't she? And my blood . . ." My next thought had my heart climbing into my throat. "Am I still human?"

"We'll await the results," said Lorcan, "before we make any decisions."

I knew my fate hung in the pudgy hands of Dr. Archibald Stanley Michaels. He knew it, too. And he couldn't meet my gaze.

They all turned to go.

"Wait!"

Only Stanley paused. He looked over his shoulder as his companions continued down the hallway.

"Please let me out," I said. "I'll stay with you in the lab and help—just like I used to."

He smiled sadly. "I have plenty of lab assistants, Libby. And none of them have ever spilled hydrochloric acid on my Bigfoot specimens."

Ouch. The acid had eaten through the hair samples, including the follicles with skin tags. We'd been this close to getting a DNA sample, and I tipped over the wrong bottle. "Please, Stanley. Get me out of here."

"I can't."

He turned to go, and I watched him get swallowed by the darkness. I couldn't see far enough down the hall to view the door. But I heard it open. And close.

I smacked the wall in frustration. They couldn't keep me here.

Not forever.

*   *   *

I had a fitful sleep and awoke, I assume, some-time during the day. All the vampires were snug in their coffins while their pet wolves prowled the town. Okay. That was a petty thought, and I didn't like being petty, even if it was deserved. I believed in karma, although I had no idea what I had done in this life or any other to get imprisoned and accused of attempted murder.

I wondered how Patrick was doing. I couldn't bear the thought of him dying. Or anyone dying, es-pecially as the result of something I had done.

Breakfast was eggs, bacon, toast, and orange juice. I drank the juice and ate the toast. I wanted badly to eat the bacon, too. Meat was nearly an aphrodisiac. I stopped just shy of licking it.

Stan knew I was vegan. Maybe he hadn't ad-justed the meals as another way to torment me on behalf of his new masters.

Resentment was a thorn piercing my conscience. I needed to stop thinking such negative thoughts.

I filled the hours doing yoga, meditation, and mantras. I practiced pranayama breathing tech-niques and incorporated a few mudras, which were spiritual gestures made with the hands. Afterward, I felt much better.

I took a very long, hot shower. I washed my panties in the sink and left them to dry on the towel rack. I wandered around in the nude while my underwear dried. I wondered who was monitoring me. Probably some sort of machine Stan had dreamed up. Maybe Mr. Roboto was more than just a voice.

Lunch was potato leek soup, sourdough bread, and iced tea. I was starving, but my first spoonful of soup revealed tiny bits of sausage.

Yum. I mean yuck.

Man, I was on the near equivalent of bread and water.

When my underwear dried, I put it on and then I donned the pajamas. I took a short nap. Then I did yoga again. I had no way to tell time, but I knew it must be close to evening.

An hour, maybe two passed. Mr. Roboto wouldn't talk to me anymore. At this point, I'd settle for chatting with Melvin. Was he still hanging around? Or had he gotten bored and flown off to haunt someone else?

No one visited. Not even Ralph. But why would he? Could I blame him for putting his sons' welfare over mine? They had already lost their mother. It must've been really hard for Ralph to raise his babies alone. Now, he was doing it undead.

The panel in the wall that delivered my meals popped open and the tray slid out. There was a white bag, a large Styrofoam cup, and a folded note. And, thank the heavens, a copy of *Reader's Digest* and of *People*.

I removed all the items. I opened the note first.

Libby,
    I made you a veggie burger with lettuce,
tomato, and onion. Condiments on the side.
(Is mayo a "by-product"? ☺) Extra-large fries.
Your chocolate shake is made with almond milk.

Ralph

I opened the bag. The burger smelled heavenly. I loaded on ketchup and mustard because yes, mayonnaise was on my animal by-product list, and devoured it along with the fries. Hmm-mmm. The chocolate shake was perfection.

It was also drugged.

When I awoke, I was strapped to a metal table. A man in surgical clothing, his face masked, bent over me. His gloved hands held a nasty-looking instrument. A big, bright light shone above me. I couldn't make out anything else in the room.

I wanted to scream, but my mouth wasn't working. My only solace was that he was putting the tool away. Fear pulsed through me, a cold, dull throb that barely penetrated my drug-numbed senses.

He seemed surprised to see me awake. I recognized him behind the thick lenses of his glasses. Stan. My lips formed his name, but there was no sound.

His betrayal wounded me. I knew, somewhere beyond where the drugs could reach, that the man standing above me so liberally experimenting on my person would pay for what he was doing.

We must've been alone. I was grateful for that, at least.

BOOM! What the hell was that? The reverberations knocked Stan to the floor. The whole place shook and the big light swung wildly.

I struggled to free myself, but the straps kept my wrists and ankles bound tightly. I couldn't be sure I was moving at all; perhaps my mind only made it seem like I was trying to escape.

Stan gripped the edge of the operating table and pulled himself to his feet. He ripped off his paper cap and mask.

"Libby!" he yelled.

Another explosion stole the rest of his words. Panic clawed at me. I was trapped. Stan would leave me. The room would cave in.

I would die.

I turned wide eyes to Stanley, knowing my terror showed in my gaze. He pulled off the wires stuck to my chest and removed the IV in my right arm. Then he grappled with the straps on my wrists. He freed my arms, then moved to unbuckle my ankles. Shakily, I rose on my elbows. The sheet covering me slid off, and I realized I was naked underneath it.

Here it was, the end of the world, and I was gonna meet my Maker in my birthday suit. Perfect.

Stanley got my left leg free, but he was Mr. Fumble Fingers as he tried to remove the strap binding my right ankle.

BOOM! BOOM! The terrifying noises erupted right above us. The light flickered and chunks of the ceiling crashed around us. Stanley ripped at the buckles.

"Just go!" I screamed. My voice was scratchy and weak, but he heard me.

"No," he said. "I won't leave you."

The strap loosened and I pulled my leg out. He looked at me, triumphant. An ominous crack sounded above, and then the ceiling gave way.

Stan didn't have time to move.

He was buried instantly.

Chapter 11

"Stan!" I screamed. My mind was still foggy, but the tender hold of the drugs slipped away. I felt terrible; my mouth tasted like metal.

I got off the table, my feet stabbed by broken glass and concrete shards. My legs folded, and I grabbed the table for support. Unbelievably, the light only dropped a couple of feet; it was still on, too.

I lowered myself to the floor and crawled to Stan. Shards pierced my palms and knees, but the pain was dulled. Sweat dripped off my temples and rolled down my neck. The acrid smell of smoke singed my nostrils. It was familiar, that scent. Like home. Like family.

I kept moving, thinking only of getting to Stan. I needed to save him, so I could strangle him later.

My heart dropped when I saw Stan's pale hand sticking out from the rocks.

Seeing my old friend, my uncle Archie, buried by debris swept aside my anger about his actions. I could browbeat him later, if he lived to hear my harangue. I wasn't leaving him in the rubble. I flung away rock after rock.

"Stan? I'm getting you out," I said. "Keep breathing. Please, just keep breathing."

The noise and explosions stopped. What had blown up the building? A gas leak? A nuclear missile? A werewolf having a bad day?

I cocked my head. I heard fire singing. It was far away, but I heard it all the same. The song was different than the others I'd heard before. It called to me. It seduced me.

But I couldn't answer. I couldn't leave Stan.

I uncovered Stan's legs and torso. Dread pounded through me. His injuries looked bad. One leg was bent at an impossible angle, and he had several broken ribs. Blood stained his clothes and seeped from jagged wounds.

I kept digging, and refused to consider that Stan wasn't alive. Whatever drug I'd been given made me feel like I'd imbibed too many Venti Mochas, and that made me think about Starbucks. What I wouldn't give for a Raspberry White Chocolate Mocha, with soy milk and no whip.

Vaguely, I wondered where everyone was. I

mean, surely they knew Stan had been going all Dr. Frankenstein on me. An unearthly stillness settled over us. The space above was completely dark, but even so, I realized it was another room. I think the prison and lab were located under the queen's mansion, basement level. Were we still there? Or had I been moved to somewhere else? Maybe everyone had evacuated. Or maybe they were dead.

No, I wouldn't think that way.

I lifted the final concrete chunk from Stan's body and threw it. It banged against the wall, and I flinched at the harsh sound.

The green outline around Stan was dimming and I didn't want to see it fade away. "C'mon, Stan! Stay with me."

The light was flickering, and I figured it would go out soon. It was just as well. The yellow beam revealed the wide, unseeing stare of my old friend. His glasses had somehow remained on his face, but the lenses were cracked.

"No," I said, shaking my finger at him. "You're not dead. Do you hear me? You're. Not. Dead."

I looked down and realized I was still naked, and sweaty and dusty, and just a little bit out of my mind. I tugged the sheet from the debris-strewn table and made a suitable toga with it. Then I got behind Stanley and lifted him by his shoulders. I dragged him from the rocks as gently as I could. He was heavy, and moving him was like trying to move a two-hundred-pound bag of rice.

Behind me, the weak beam of the downed light revealed a door. I headed toward it with my precious cargo. I only laid down my burden long enough to pull the handle.

It was locked.

I yanked and yanked, but the goddamned door wouldn't open. I screamed and pounded on the metal until my voice went hoarse and my hands went numb.

Exhausted, I pulled Stan to the corner and collapsed next to him. That was the moment the light blinked out. Darkness blanketed the entire room. I stroked Stan's forehead and promised him everything would be okay. This was a lie, of course. But Stan didn't appear to care.

I drifted in and out of consciousness. Then, from far away, I heard a familiar voice.

"Libby!"

"Here," I croaked; my throat sore. "Here!"

"Don't worry," said Ralph on the other side of the door. "We'll get you out."

"Hurry," I said. "Stan is really hurt."

"Move out of the way!" yelled a fierce female voice.

The door burst off its hinges and flew across the room. I blinked as bobbing lights headed in my direction. I realized several people had filed into the room, and they held flashlights. One was a short, stacked redhead who marched toward us with fire in her eyes.

"He's not dead," she told me matter-of-factly. She knelt next to Stan and rubbed the bald spot on his head. "He'll be just fine."

"Linda," said another, softer Irish voice. I made out the tall shape of a woman. Her skin glimmered strangely. "We must help Libby. Stanley is—"

"Fine. Stanley is fine." Linda scooped Stan into her arms and lifted him as if he weighed no more than air. "Brigid, as soon as you're done tending to the girl, you come and fix up my man."

Then she stomped out of the room.

Ralph sat down next to me. His blue eyes were filled with relief. His fingers swept my hair back from my forehead.

I felt so relieved to be alive. "What's going on? Is Stan . . . oh, God!"

Ralph's response was unexpected. He kissed me. Talk about bad timing. His lips were warm and soft and tasted like cinnamon. Heat spread through my body. It was like we shared the fire again, and I reveled in that feeling.

I clutched at his shirt and let the tears flow. Gently, he moved back and wiped off my gritty cheeks. I looked like hell and probably tasted like asphalt, and he planted one on me anyway.

The sparkly woman knelt next to me. Her

diaphanous gown was green and showed off her lithe frame. "My name is Brigid. I'm a healer, and I can help you."

I studied her, feeling tired and scared. Glittery gold symbols on her skin swirled and changed patterns. "Those are some crazy tattoos."

"My magic knows what you need." Okay. That made no sense, but what was new? Nothing in Broken Heart made sense. Brigid put her cool, soothing palm against my forehead. "Sleep well, Libby."

That was the last thing I remembered.

I awoke in darkness. The bed underneath me was really comfortable and the sheets were so soft I felt wrapped in clouds. Huh. I must've gotten an upgraded prison cell.

Yay me.

I was really tired of getting knocked out and waking up in strange places. Seriously. What was wrong with these people?

I stretched, relieved I was dressed in pajamas. These fit me better, too. Overall, I felt good. My body didn't hurt at all, and the buzzing headache that had plagued me when I awoke on Stan's surgical table was completely gone. Whatever Brigid the Glitter Girl had done, it was miraculous.

I tried not to think about Stan, but how could I not? He was dead. I was sorry, too, even though he'd been experimenting on me. And he didn't exactly stop his new pals from treating me so poorly. I had lots of reasons to be mad at Stan, but I didn't want him dead.

And what about Patrick? Surely they'd figured out I wasn't responsible for his sickness. Without Stan to do the testing, how would I be proven innocent? I could only hope Patrick was already recovering.

"Lights on, fifty percent," I muttered to Mr. Roboto.

Nothing happened.

"Lights on, fifty percent," I said louder.

"You have to flip the switch," said Ralph's amused voice.

"Aaaaahhh!" I sat up and pulled the covers over my head, which was stupid. How was a comforter going to shield me from anything?

A light snapped on as I cautiously lowered the bedspread. Ralph stood in the doorway looking at me, his blue eyes filled with apprehension.

"And I thought I slept like the dead," he said.

"Oh, hah." I was nervous. This was not a prison; this was someone's bedroom.

"Mine," he said, answering the question before I could ask it. "I took responsibility for you."

"They wanted to throw me back in the clink, didn't they?"

"We have to protect ourselves," he defended.

Then he sighed and rubbed a hand through his hair. "Stan shouldn't have—"

"Experimented on me?"

He nodded. "And even after he did, you saved him."

And it looked like Ralph had saved me. Again. But why? He'd made it clear he didn't like what was happening to me. To him. To us.

"Thanks." I didn't want to look at him anymore, not when I couldn't hide how I felt. I didn't care if it was the dragon fire, the magic that bound us. I liked him. I wanted him.

I studied the room. The sleigh bed was dark cherry wood. The sheets were gold lined with red, which the comforter's swirling pattern matched perfectly. The nightstands matched the rich wood of the bed, as did the dresser and armoire. There were no windows; the walls had an odd silver sheen.

Yep. I was in the vampire's lair.

Still, it was filled with a married couple's furniture. Oy. I couldn't help but think about Ralph and his wife going to the furniture store and picking it all out. They'd probably made love in this bed, and he'd slept next to her every night while their twins grew in her womb.

I felt self-conscious sleeping in her bed. Like I was the Other Woman.

"What's wrong?" he asked. "Are you okay?"

"What do you think?" My harsh tone made him

flinch. Crap. How could I explain what I was feeling without sounding like an idiot? I smiled weakly. "Your wife had good taste in bedroom suites."

"Therese didn't . . . that is, this set belonged to my parents. After she passed away, I sold our old suite and took all this out of storage." He examined me, as if trying to figure out what else I might want to know. "The bedding was a gift from my sister. And the pajamas you're wearing are new. I guessed your size."

I hadn't even thought about where the pajamas had come from. "I didn't mean to freak. It's just weird. You being a widower. I feel like I'm intruding." I paused. "You bought me new pajamas?"

"Sorry. They were a gift from Patsy."

I was a little disappointed Ralph hadn't picked them out for me. Gah. I was so pathetic.

"I'll make you breakfast," he said.

I glanced at him and noticed his fangs were extended. I put a hand to my throat and gulped.

"What?" I squeaked.

"Not like that," he said impatiently. "I meant I'll cook for you, and then we can go."

"Go where?"

"The queen has called a council meeting." His gaze bounced away guiltily. "I'm supposed to take you there."

"Wait a minute." I glared at him. "You're my jailer now?"

"I told you. The only way to keep you out of that place was to agree to be your . . . escort." He looked at me, stone-faced. "Do you know what that means?"

My heart stuttered. "If I escape . . . you mean they'd kill you?"

"Worse." He stared at me, and his lips thinned. "They'd taunt me. I'd never live down letting a human escape my evil vampire clutches."

I didn't know if I should laugh or throw a pillow at him. I settled for a smile.

I could always smack him later.

Lucky for me, the vampires laundered my clothes and gave them to Ralph. After a quick shower, I got dressed and brushed out my hair, then I French-braided it.

I went to the kitchen, feeling once again out of place. This was the home he'd made with Therese and their sons. I didn't feel like I belonged.

"Where are your boys?"

"They're staying with my in-laws in California. It's safer for them there. And no, they don't know about my condition."

"Are things really that dangerous here?"

"You were here for five minutes and got attacked by two wolves, a Tainted vampire, and a zombie. Then two dragons fell out of the sky."

"Ah. Good point."

After that, Ralph and I didn't have much to say to each other. While he made pancakes, I wandered his house. It was a small two-bedroom bungalow that Ralph kept tidy. With his sons here, I bet it wasn't nearly as easy to keep clean. I imagined clothing and toys and books strewn from the front yard to their bedroom. I found the idea enchanting, and for a strange moment I yearned to know what it was like, chasing after two giggling three-year-olds.

I stood in the doorway of the twins' room, and marveled. The walls were sky blue, and the border around the top featured brightly colored trains. Two toddler-sized beds in the shape of cabooses were neatly made up; each small pillow had a brown teddy bear. Those fuzzy fellows waited for the return of their tiny playmates. I wondered how long it would be before they came back, and how long it would be before they could live here safely with their father. Maybe never. Even though I was upset with Ralph, I couldn't help but feel sad for him.

I flicked off the light and returned to the kitchen, where Ralph was putting the finishing touches on breakfast.

I was so nervous about the meeting that I didn't really have an appetite. I ate the pancakes because Ralph had gone to the trouble of making them. It seemed a thousand years ago that I was sneaking into Broken Heart to find proof of the paranormal.

"Do you know what happened to my cell phone?" I asked.

"Confiscated," he said.

"Do you have one?"

"You can't call anyone. Not yet."

I really wanted to call my parents. I wanted to hear Mom's voice. It might've been childish to want my mommy, but I wasn't going to deny I'd be relieved to see her and Dad again. I wanted to protect them, especially if they'd gotten clear of the town. I was worried. If they'd given up trying to find me, then PRIS would descend on Broken Heart.

I had so many questions about what was going on, what had happened to me. But all I could think about were those two empty beds and those two lonely teddy bears.

"When will you see your boys again?" I asked as we cleaned up the breakfast dishes. The window above the kitchen sink showed that it was pitch-black outside. I must've slept all day. Keeping a vampire's hours already; I might as well get used to it.

"Visits are difficult to manage," he said. "I told you my in-laws don't know I'm a vampire. They think I work for the Consortium as a project manager, and that I've been sent out of the country on a special assignment."

My heart broke for him. "So, you don't get to see them at all?"

"Every Sunday," he said. "My computer has a webcam, and my in-laws have the same setup. We do see each other. It's not the same as having them within arm's reach, but it'll have to do."

"Why stay here?" I asked. "You could take the boys and start over somewhere else. Get out of this place. I mean, it's crazy here. Look at what happened last night." I blinked at my own statement. "What did happen last night?"

"Broken Heart has had some problems," said Ralph. "One of them is named Lia, and she showed up last night on her dragon. That thing blew the hell out of the mansion and destroyed Stan's lab."

"You mean the blue dragon? The one that killed his sister?"

"Unfortunately, no. We don't know who he is."

"And this Lia person?"

"She's an Ancient."

I stared at him blankly. He nodded. "Right. The short version is that there are seven Ancient vampires, the original ones who created all the vampires we have now. Every Family has a different power."

"Like you with the fire thing."

He nodded. "Anyway, Lia's an Ancient. And she's not happy about Patsy's leadership."

"Patsy led a coup?"

Ralph laughed. "Hell, no. She got sucked in because of a prophecy. Basically, it said the Ancients' way of doing things would end, and Patsy would be the new vampire queen, and oh yeah, lead the lycanthropes, too. Not that the werewolves are exactly paying her tribute."

"She said something about that before," I said, trying to figure out where to put all the pieces of the Broken Heart puzzle. Damn. I was never very good at putting together puzzles.

"So, anyway, a few months ago, Lia conspired with two other Ancients. She was the one staging a coup. It failed."

I was beginning to see why Ralph had sent his sons out of the state. How the hell could all this paranormal drama unfold without anyone in the real world noticing? Broken Heart was a small town, and it was plunked in the middle of nowhere. No one would come here on purpose. Lots of paranormal rumors were flying around, which is why my parents and I had decided to check it out. I wondered what Broken Heart's citizens had done—and were still willing to do—to protect their secrets.

"I'm sorry about Stan," said Ralph, mistaking the reason for my silence. I probably should've been more worried about Stan's actions. I suppose it didn't matter all that much since he was . . . dead. I wasn't sure how to feel about it. I really didn't want to think about him or what happened.

But apparently Ralph did.

"We didn't know he'd taken you to do other tests. That's why we couldn't find you at first."

"How did you find me?"

"Melvin. He found Patsy and gave the search party directions."

"I guess I owe him one." I felt strange about that. I wondered if the ghost was here now. Feeling foolish, I said, "Uh . . . thanks, Melvin."

Ralph chuckled. "I don't think the spirits are with us."

"Shut up. I'll have you know he likes me."

"He's not the only one," he said softly.

"What was that?"

"Nothing." He looked down at the sink and an awkward silence fell between us.

"What about Patrick?" I asked. "Is he okay?"

"I don't know," said Ralph. "But I don't believe his illness has anything to do with you."

I appreciated his confidence, but as it turned out, he was wrong.

Apparently the meeting would convene at the queen's mansion, which looked beat up, but by no means in danger of falling apart. The attack had obviously been directed at the middle of the large house. The brick walls were blackened, but solid. The roof had been tarped and broken windows had been covered with plywood.

The front door no longer existed, but the two big wolves, both outlined in red, standing guard at the entrance were better security anyway. They both growled at me as we passed. I resisted the urge to stick out my tongue. Ralph kept a firm grip on my hand. I pretended he wanted the romantic connection even though he probably just wanted to keep me from running away. What he didn't know is that I'd already figured out running away was a bad idea. Not just because I would be hunted by scary paranormal creatures, but because, so far, running away from my problems had only made 'em worse.

After getting a "sniff and nod" from the guards, we entered the house. The smell of burned wood and melted plastic assailed me. I saw Ralph's nose twitch and realized the scent was probably a hundred times worse for him.

The large staircase was broken and burned. The lower part was completely gone. A hole at least twenty feet across had been blown out, and far below was Stanley's destroyed lab. I didn't get a chance to really look because Ralph hustled me down a wide hallway and into a formal dining room. The long table could easily seat forty people, and almost half the chairs were full. Patsy was seated at the head and Gabriel to her right. And to her left . . .

"Stan!" I stared at him, unable to believe my own eyes. He didn't look like he'd been crushed by a fallen ceiling. He didn't have a cut on him, and he wasn't wearing his glasses, either. I hurried forward, ignoring all the people at the table. I didn't know them, and probably wouldn't like them anyway.

"It is you!" I hugged him. "You're alive!"

"Well, not quite," he said. "I'm a vampire."

"And he's married," said the redheaded woman, who stood up next to him and wrapped her possessive arm around his. Stan looked so happy he was about to burst.

His wife gave me a perfectly manicured hand, but her gaze wasn't all that friendly. "I'm Linda Michaels."

"Libby Monroe." I looked at Stan. Now that he was walking around again, I could go back to being pissed-off at him. "Why'd you experiment on me?"

The silence was sudden, and I could feel everyone's gazes on us.

Stan had the grace to look ashamed. "I needed samples."

"You had to strap me down to a table to get blood?"

"I did the blood tests. Your liver function test was off the charts. I had to be sure."

"And you couldn't ask me?" It was awkward, the three of us standing and chatting while fifteen or so other people stared at us. I was well aware that the queen was indulging me, and that I could easily end up back in a cell, or worse.

"I wasn't sure you would cooperate," he said. "Maybe it was the coward's way, Libby, but I did what I thought was best. I had hoped to get the necessary samples before you woke up."

What in the hell had Stanley found in my blood work that made him drug me and perform procedures without my permission? Anxiety rippled, and I started to worry. Was I sick? Did I have some kind of heinous new disease capable of killing vampires? Was it as I secretly feared—the dragon had irrevocably changed me?

"You didn't have the right," I said as fear gnawed away at my caution. "None of you had the right to experiment on me! To toss me in jail! How dare you just . . . just confiscate my life!"

Tears spilled, and I didn't care. Let them see my weakness. To them, I was a mere human, worth nothing. How easy it was for these creatures to hold me hostage, to unravel all that I had worked for because it suited their purposes. I felt anger coil, the familiar heat spread through me. They thought what I had done in the living room was bad? Hah!

"Why, Stanley?" I yelled, feeling the power grow inside me. I shaped my fury, held on to it, waited to unleash it. "What's so wrong with me?"

"Libby," said Stanley, his voice rife with concern. "You're not human."

Chapter 12

His words cooled my anger as quickly as water thrown onto a fire. The fury dissipated, replaced quickly with hurt. I put my hands on my hips.

"What do you mean? I was human two days ago."

"Before the dragon kissed you."

"Why don't you go sit down by Ralph?" asked Patsy. "And we'll start the meeting."

By which she meant witch trial, I was sure. I walked to the chair that Ralph pulled out for me and sat. He didn't look at me, but his hand found mine under the table. I appreciated the comfort. I wasn't really mad at him anymore; because of him I had some freedom. He'd invited me into his house, into his life, and I hadn't exactly been grateful.

"We're all here now, so let's start with Stanley's enthusiastic if unauthorized research results," said Patsy. I appreciated the censure in her voice. At least she hadn't agreed with Stan's experimentation on my unconscious self.

"Since my lab is destroyed," said Stan, "I don't have the data. However, based on the initial blood work, which I hoped to confirm with other testing, it appears Libby is not human. Rather, she is not all human."

I shook my head. Getting turned into a bloodsucker, or maybe it was just getting KOed by the ceiling, had scrambled Stan's brains. How could I not be all human?

"What is she?" asked Lorcan. "Something like the *loup de sang*? A hybrid?"

"Yes, a hybrid," said Stan. He cleared his throat, looking nervous. "Again, I need further testing to gain proof, but I believe she's . . . part dragon."

Reactions were varied. Some laughed, others consulted those nearest to them, and still others peered at me as if I would sprout scales and breathe fire.

"What about Ralph?" asked one man with thick, black hair and jade green eyes. His German accent was pronounced. Oh, yes. The mean man who'd come to the jail the day before. On either side of him were men who were his dopplegängers. Triplets. Oh, great. Like one wasn't scary enough.

"I ran blood tests on Ralph and they both have the same . . . quirks."

"And yet, he didn't strap you to a table and poke you with sharp instruments," I said in a low voice.

"Would it make you feel better if he had?"

"A little."

"Dragons? Really?" Patsy's voice echoed with shock. Nearly everyone at the table looked as discombobulated as she did.

"Yes," said Stan. "Dragons are rare. We have to assume there is a reason two came to Broken Heart. And one gave her powers to Libby."

"Dragons. Terrific. *Not*," said Zerina, rolling her pink eyes.

Linda snorted. "Who's the one who licks trees 'round here?"

"That was a tree nymph!" said Zee. She flicked her finger at Linda's head and her red hair turned purple.

"Zee!" yelled Patsy. "Change it back. Now."

Zerina flicked her finger again, and in a second Linda's hair had been returned to normal. The vampire glared at the fairy.

"That's enough, children. The adults would like to talk now," said Patsy. Her tone brooked no argument.

At this table sat proof of bloodsuckers, shape-shifters, fairies, and heaven knew what else. All the same, it seemed silly to think that me—a plain ol' human—could somehow be turned into a dragon.

"Other than the blood work, I have reason to believe my theory is correct," said Stan.

Oh, no. He was going to out my and Ralph's little fire dance. I wanted to stall him, but I couldn't think of anything to say.

"Libby and Ralph both show a proclivity for fire manipulation."

It wasn't quite the bombshell I was expecting. The others didn't seem all that impressed, either.

"Do you think Libby's powers might be inherited?" asked Patsy. "Maybe she already had some dragon blood and, when the other woman died, she activated it somehow?"

"It wouldn't explain Ralph's sudden powers," said Stan, sounding a little defensive.

"He's from Hu Mua Lan's line," said Gabriel. "Fire is his power."

"Well," said Stan. He shrugged, his lips curving into a grin. "Libby's mother always said she was half alien."

"Look, Mom and Dad experimented with peyote that night," I said before Stan could launch into Mom's well-known account of her abduction. "Dad woke up in a tree. After he climbed out of it, he found Mom wandering in the New Mexico desert, naked and delirious."

"You don't believe your mother's story?" asked Patsy.

All eyes turned to me. I hesitated. Mom was the definition of eccentric, but she wasn't stupid or insane. I refused to let these people believe she was a crackpot.

"Of course I believe her. She said vampires, werewolves, ghosts, and fairies were real. Why not aliens?"

Patsy's steady blue gaze made me squirm.

"How could I be an alien?" I said, feeling defensive. "I was born the same as all human babies." Not in a hospital, mind you, but by a midwife in a shaman's hut in New Mexico. Still, I came out from my mother's womb.

"Relax, hon. Nobody believes you're an alien," said Patsy. "Is there any way to prove our dragon theory?"

"More tests, specifically with Libby's DNA. It would also be helpful to have actual dragon DNA for comparison."

"I know someone who can help with that," said a dark-haired man sitting next to Lorcan. They looked a lot alike, but he seemed a little older than Lorcan and his eyes weren't as shadowed by suspicion.

"What monkey are we asking to join our circus now, Ruadan?" Patsy rubbed her belly.

"Her name is Ash."

"The soul shifter?" said Zerina. "Are you insane?"

"Like Stan said, dragons are rare, and those who hunt them rarer still. If anyone can help us, it's her."

"Okay," said Patsy. "Let's get her here. What about the tests, Stan?"

"No," I said. I pointed a finger at Stan. "And if I wake up on a table being carved up like a Thanksgiving turkey again, I'll kill you."

A chair scooted back and Linda popped up, her death stare aimed at me. Her mouth opened, but before she could utter a word Patsy held up a hand.

"Sit down and stick a cork in it." She pointed at Stan and Linda. Stan looked embarrassed, but Linda's expression was pure pissed-off. They both sat down. "Libby is our reluctant guest, and I don't blame her for not wanting to get poked and prodded.

"Problem is, we drained Patrick dry as dust and refilled him with fresh donor blood. He's still not doing well, which means neither is Jess. If Libby's blood is poisonous to vampires, we need to know for sure. Then we need to figure out how to counteract it."

Murmurs of agreement rumbled from the others. I hated the idea that my blood might be poisonous. It was a terrible thing to know that trying to make up for one mistake only made everything worse.

Ralph squeezed my hand and I looked into his reassuring gaze. He was boyishly handsome, his blue eyes as warm as a spring day. I drew strength from him. He smiled and the mere curve of his lips sent my pulse racing.

"Libby, my name is Eva O'Halloran. I'm the schoolteacher," said a soft female voice. The woman was pretty, with dark hair and kind eyes. She sat close to Lorcan, whose arm was around her shoulders. His silver eyes regarded me with suspicion.

She asked, "Is your mother Theodora Maribelle Monroe?"

"Yes," I said. "How did you know that?" My stomach clenched. How did they know my parents? Were they in jeopardy?

"My husband and I run the library, too. Is your mother the one who wrote *Werewolves Are Real!*"

Ah. They knew Mom was an author. I relaxed a little.

"Yes, and she also wrote *Vampires Are Real! Ghosts Are Real! Bigfoot Is Real!* and so on," I said. My mother owned and operated Liberty Press (yes, named after me, ack!), so she published her work whenever she liked. She employed professional editors, printers, and cover artists. Her books had even hit a few independent bookstores' bestseller lists. She had a cult following in some parts of the country.

"Don't forget *Aliens Are Real!*" said Stan.

"Ah," said Eva. "I haven't read that one." She

turned to Patsy. "Maybe we should invite Mr. and Mrs. Monroe to Broken Heart. They may be a valuable resource."

"We've been compromised enough. Bringing paranormal investigators to the town is unwise," advised Gabriel.

No kidding. I needed to know if my parents were all right and I desperately wanted to let them know I was okay, too.

Patsy leaned toward Gabriel. They had a whispered conversation. Everyone else tried not to look at me. I wanted to click my heels three times and wish myself out of here. *There's no place like home, there's no place like—*

"Libby," Patsy finally said. I looked up, my heart kicking into overdrive. Ralph squeezed my hand again. "Would you please consider giving the samples Stan needs to conduct further testing? The lives of our two friends may well depend on the results."

"I have a choice?" I asked suspiciously.

She nodded.

"And if I say no?"

"Then no one will touch you." She gave Stan a significant look. He flinched.

Naturally, all eyes were drawn to me again, and I felt the weight of those stares. I looked at Ralph, wishing I could to talk to him. He really was my only ally; I wondered if he could be more than that.

Ralph waited patiently, his gaze telling me what his lips couldn't. He supported me. He thought I was worthwhile. He wanted what was best for me.

Well, at least that's what I imagined he was thinking. He kept a firm grip on my hand, and nodded at me. He was still smiling, and just knowing he was in my corner made me feel like everything was going to be okay.

"I hurt Patrick unintentionally," I said carefully. "I didn't think about my actions, and for that I'm sorry. I don't know if I am responsible for Patrick's condition. I mean, the whole thing is hard to believe." I inhaled a deep breath and nearly squeezed Ralph's hand right off. "If the key to saving Patrick and Jessica is locked inside my DNA, then yes, I'll submit to more tests."

Patsy smiled, and I felt like a student who'd gotten the teacher's approval.

"I have only two conditions," I said, regretting that my words made her smile disappear. I really wanted to stay on the good side of the queen.

"All right," said Patsy. Her tone was cautious. "What do you want?"

"I want to call my parents. They need to know I'm all right."

Patsy nodded. "I'll allow it, but you can't tell them about us. And you have to make sure they don't come to Broken Heart."

God. What would they do if they knew my

parents had already been wandering around? I didn't want to think about it.

"And the second condition?"

"I want an advocate. Someone who will look out for my interests. And I want this person to stay with me during the testing."

"You're telling us you want a lawyer?" drawled Patsy. She was amused by my request. Well, my request might be funny to her, but she was sitting at the head of the table, loved, protected, and honored. I was the bug crawling under everyone else's raised shoes. I knew very well what my fate might be once my usefulness had ended.

"I don't care what his or her profession is," I countered. "I want someone who gives a damn about what happens to me."

Patsy looked as though she'd been slapped, and I was glad. I cast my gaze around the table. "I'm not important to any of you. I'm just a . . . a nuisance. Everyone here could swat me like a buzzing fly and think no more about it."

"I see your point," said Patsy, her voice quieting the murmurs of protest. "We value life, Libby, though we may have infringed on yours. I assure we have no intention of killing you."

I guess I should've felt relieved, but words were not actions. I didn't trust them. "Can I have an advocate?"

"I'm reluctant to bring in outsiders," she said.

"Is there no one here you would consider your advocate?"

My gaze went immediately to Ralph. I wanted him to be my champion. In so many ways, he already was. I didn't want to think of him as my warden anymore.

He looked at me for a long time, his gaze offering me no clue to his thoughts. Then he turned to Patsy and said, "I'll do it. I'll be Libby's advocate."

Chapter 13

Ralph took me into the foyer and handed me a cell phone. "It's disposable. And untraceable."

"You guys are really paranoid."

"For good reason."

I took the phone and flipped it open.

"Keep it short," he reminded me.

"I know," I said. It wasn't like I hadn't just been told the forty-two or so rules about making this call. "I only tell them I'm okay and I'll be in touch soon." I glanced at him. "I will, won't I?"

"Yes," he said without hesitation. "I'll make sure of it."

His confidence made me feel better. I wasn't sure how things were going to work out here, but at least the Consortium wanted to keep me alive. We had that goal in common.

I dialed my mother's cell phone number. It went immediately to voice mail. Not good. Mom always answered her phone. She never wanted to miss the one tip that might bag us something supernatural. I didn't leave a message because I didn't want it to count as my phone call.

"She's not picking up. I'll try my father."

I had a choice. Dial my dad's cell and hope he answered. Or call Braddock Hayes, PRIS team leader, who was in Texas on another case. He'd joined us about ten years ago, not long after we lost Stan at the nightwalker farm. Brady was a former employee of a government agency he never named. He brought with him black-bag skills and technology that seemed plucked from the latest science fiction novels. He usually ran things from the command center, but he also had created and trained an elite team of investigators who took on the more covert operations. Truth be told, he intimidated the hell out of me.

The pit of my stomach felt hollow. What if Mom and Dad weren't all right? Worry gnawed at me, but I was still reluctant to tell Ralph or his friends that my parents might be in trouble.

"Everything okay?" asked Ralph.

"Yeah." I punched numbers into the phone. "I'm going to try one more time." The phone started ringing. I scowled at Ralph. "Do you mind?"

Regret passed over his face. "Sorry, Libby."

"I get it. You have to make sure I don't violate Patsy's rules." I was disappointed, though. Not only because he didn't trust me, but also because he had good reason not to. I wanted someone at PRIS to know where I was and rescue me. But mostly, I wanted confirmation my parents were alive and well.

"Hayes." My eyes welled up upon my hearing a familiar voice. It wasn't Mom or Dad, but I'd take what I could get.

"Hi, Dad," I said, turning away from Ralph. I tried to keep my breathing even while I concentrated on keeping my heart rate steady. I didn't need my human reactions giving away my deception to the vampire.

"Liberty. Stats," he said.

That was Brady for you, all business. I knew he'd go with the lie immediately and would also know something wasn't on the up and up. We had member-protection protocols, which had been developed and implemented by Brady. Mom and Dad's loose style of running PRIS had tightened up considerably thanks to Brady. No one wanted to lose another member of our team, not like we had lost Stan.

"Is Mom around?" I asked. "I couldn't get her on the phone."

"Your mother's out shopping. Her cell's been acting up." He was saying my parents hadn't checked in or returned. Same as me. "When are you coming back, pumpkin?"

Oh, please. Brady trying to be affectionate was like Simon Cowell trying to give a compliment.

"I'm doing research and decided to hang out for a while." I swallowed the knot in my throat.

"In Broken Heart?"

"Claremore. Broken Heart was a bust." We used this phrase to confirm the opposite. Now Brady knew where I was and that there was lots of interesting stuff here.

"Your mom will probably want to call you back. Is your cell still giving you problems?"

"Yeah. Reception out here is really bad. Had to use a pay phone." I'd just told him my communication options were limited.

"I see." He paused. "Do you need anything?"

Despite my efforts to stay calm, my heart skipped a beat and my stomach squeezed. He'd asked the question we used as code for: Do you need help? Here was the part when I let him know my status.

"I'd love some chocolate."

"You and your truffles," he said, laughing. God, he was good at deception. "Dark, milk, or white?"

More code words. Dark meant I needed immediate assistance. Milk indicated I was safe for now, but I wanted backup. If I said white, then he would know I wasn't in danger, just being cautious, and would be in touch in twenty-four hours.

"You know milk chocolate is my favorite," I responded. He was in Houston, about ten hours away. I knew Brady would drive because getting his gizmos through airport security was impossible. Plus, he was strangely paranoid about the Transportation Security Administration.

We said good-bye. I shouldn't have felt guilty for telling Brady to come to Broken Heart. But I was scared. I didn't know what was happening to me—all the weird stuff with fire and the near obsessive attraction to Ralph. I didn't know how long the queen and her cronies planned to keep me. But most of all, I didn't know what had happened to my parents. I needed to know they were okay.

PRIS was my family. And they were coming to rescue me.

In Ralph's Honda, we followed Stan's minivan to a big, white RV parked in a vacant, well-lit parking lot. An old basketball court was a few yards away from a razed area. Soccer goals occupied the far end of the field.

"Used to be the high school," said Ralph as we got out of the car. He took my hand, which so gave me the warm fuzzies, as he led me to the edge of the blacktop. We stared at the place where the building once stood. "It got blown up last summer."

"Seems to be a lot of that going around."

"Yeah." He sighed. "I'm not sure how safe it is for

the grown-ups, much less our kids. The children attend school in the compound now, which is at least semisafe."

"Eva's their only teacher?" I asked.

"Yes. We don't have a lot of students. The Consortium built the compound for its headquarters, but it turned out to be the only secure place in town. Patsy's been dismantling the wall around it and trying to get the residents to use the businesses and homes again.

"That was the whole reason the Consortium came here, to create a community for parakind to live and work. It would be nice to live in a town where the other residents understood each other's natures."

"I think that's the hope in every town," I said. "It's a great idea, though. I never thought about how difficult it would be for paranormal beings to hide in the world of humans."

"Yeah. If only the bad guys didn't drop by every couple of months to cause hell for us." He sighed as he turned to look at me. "I think I'd give almost anything to be human again. I want to have a normal life. I never thought that taking my boys to the park on a sunny day would be something I'd never do again."

My heart panged for him. I brought his knuckles to my lips and kissed them. He gathered me into his arms and looked down at me. Oh, he was so cute.

My whole body seemed to cry, "He's the *one*." I believed it. *Sigh.* Wasn't it just my luck that the guy who finally made me tingle in all the right places was dead?

"How did it happen?" I asked. "How did you become a vampire?"

I felt his shudder. He dropped his arms and moved back, his gaze on the field before us. "I had tucked the boys into bed and gone into the living room to study. I was still taking my courses to become a paramedic. After a while, I needed a breather, so I stepped outside.

"Michael and Stephen had left toys in the front yard. I started picking them up, tossing them on the porch. I heard this noise and turned around. I thought it was Bigfoot. I couldn't comprehend what I was seeing, and it was too late to run. He slammed me against my front door and tore open my neck.

"I remember a lot of pain and then I passed out. When I woke up, I was a vampire."

"Wait a minute. Bigfoot turned you into a vampire?"

Ralph laughed. "No. The creature was a vampire, but one suffering the side effects of a radical cure for the Taint. He was cured, but he attacked eleven of us, all single parents. Then the Consortium saved us, packed up all the other human residents, and just . . . took over."

He sounded resentful. I didn't blame him. I

touched his arm, and he took my hand again. His eyes were filled with turmoil. "For the second time in my life, my choice had been taken from me."

"What was the first time?"

"When I lost Therese. She got a headache. I gave her some Advil, rubbed her shoulders. She went to lie down and never woke up." His voice was tender and I realized he must've loved her very much. "An aneurysm. She was gone before the ambulance arrived. The hardest thing I've ever had to do was tell my sons their mother was never coming home."

I hadn't yet faced a moment when someone else's decision had fundamentally affected my life.

I froze.

What was I thinking? That's exactly what had happened to me. The dragon had kissed me and gave me fire magic. Patsy and her minions had taken away my choices, too. And I had been affected deeply. But something wonderful had come out of it: Ralph.

"Libby?" called Stan.

We turned around. Stan waited by the door of the RV. He had asked his wife not to accompany us, probably thinking she'd figure out a way to claw out my eyes. I didn't really expect her to be grateful I'd dug her husband out of the rocks, but still, you'd think she wouldn't be so . . . ferocious. In an odd way, I admired her loyalty; I wondered what it would be like to be loved by someone that much.

Stan led us into the RV's gleaming, well-stocked laboratory. I sat on a stool and watched Stan prepare what he needed to take samples. Ralph stood nearby, just an arm's length away.

"I thought the hospital had all the bells and whistles you need," said Ralph. "Why are we here?"

"The workers over there play with my toys," said Stan. "And break them. Do you know how long it takes to replace a gas chromatography-mass spectrometer?"

"I can't pronounce it, much less figure out how to replace it," said Ralph.

"Exactly. So I do my more sensitive work here." He looked at me. "This is where I worked full-time before the other lab was built. I kinda missed it in a weird way."

"I miss a lot of things, too, Uncle Archie," I said. "Mostly being able to make my own decisions."

He shut up.

I didn't really want to play nice. Just because he'd gotten away with carving on me and I'd saved his life (sorta) didn't mean we were going to be pals again.

Stan withdrew several vials of blood, swabbed my cheek twice, and yanked out a few strands of hair.

"Ow." I rubbed my scalp. "Aren't you gonna pull Ralph's hair, too?"

"Yep." Stan reached over and plucked a few of Ralph's locks.

"Gee, thanks." Ralph scratched his head.

"I'll need blood, too. And cheek swabs."

After he was done tormenting me and Ralph, Stan stood back. "That should do it. I hope to isolate what in your blood has affected Patrick. And figure out if your DNA has changed."

"Do you really believe . . . we're part dragon?"

"Yes. I think you believe it, too."

All this talk about me being hybrid, any kind of freaking hybrid, made me want to talk to my mom. She always knew how to comfort me.

"I don't know a lot about dragons," said Stan. "Like Ruadan said, they're rare. You know, Libby, the thing I most admired about your parents was how open they were to the supernatural possibilities. I thought you would be, too."

"Don't tell me how to feel about this," I said. "I've spent my whole life studying the paranormal world. It's one thing to hope for it, and another to see it with your own eyes. And now you're telling me I'm paranormal."

"You should be thrilled," said Stan.

"And you should've been blown up." Ralph put his hand on my shoulder and I calmed down. I sucked in a breath. "I'm sorry, Stan. I'm glad you're not dead. Well, you know what I mean."

Even so, whatever friendship we might've

resurrected had died on the surgical table, the one he put me on without asking.

Was being a dragon so ridiculous? More ridiculous than falling in lust with a vampire or living in a town run by the *loup de sang*, or even being attacked by dragons?

"Can we go?" I asked Ralph. "I don't like it in here."

"Sure." Ralph ushered me out of the lab, and Stan followed us. He opened the door and I stepped out, happy to be free of the claustrophobic RV.

"How long until you get the results?" I asked.

"A few hours."

"That's fast," I said. "Doesn't it normally take much longer to do those kinds of tests?"

"Not with my equipment." Stan touched my shoulder. I turned to look at him. "I'm sorry, Libby. I really am. For everything."

I wanted to forgive him, but I couldn't. Maybe I just needed more time.

"I appreciate what you're saying," I said. That's all I could give him, and he seemed to realize he wasn't getting absolution.

I followed Ralph off the stairs. Behind us, I heard the door shut. No more lab, needles, poking, or prodding. Tension drained, and I sighed with relief.

Ralph looked at me. "How are you feeling?"

"I'm okay. Thanks." I got the warm fuzzies all

over again. He really was my advocate. I blinked at him. "Hey . . . uh, you're getting a little fangy."

"Sorry. I haven't eaten yet." He looked at me, then at the Honda. "Do you mind stopping at my donor's?"

I didn't want him to starve, even though breakfast for Ralph would be a tasty human. He would be gnawing on someone's neck. I was kinda jealous.

"Sure. As long as I don't have to watch."

"No problem."

We walked toward the car.

"I meant to ask how you got the windshield replaced so fast."

"Simone Sweet. She runs the garage. She keeps lots of replacement parts on hand."

I heard the soft, low sounds of music. Fire singing, and it was familiar. Yes. The same music I'd heard during the blast that killed Stan.

Ralph stopped walking, then turned to me, his gaze questioning.

"I hear it, too," I said.

A red dragon swooped out of the sky. With one big, fiery breath, it blew up Stan's white minivan.

The blast threw us to the ground. Coughing and wheezing, I sat up. I was shaken and gritty, but not hurt. The same could not be said for Ralph. I scrabbled toward him and checked his carotid pulse.

Oh, right. No pulse.

"That was Linda's van!" Stan was hanging out of

the RV door. His gaze was on the destroyed vehicle. "She's gonna kill me."

"Not if the dragon does first," I called. What an idiot.

The dragon turned its big, horned head in the direction of the RV. The creature was the size of a bus. Its red scales shimmered in the firelight. Its aura was black. I could discern it from the night sky easily. Dragon vision? Whoa.

The heat from the fire rolled over me. The odd music blared, rising and flowing and beckoning. *We are one*, it whispered seductively. *Join with me, daughter. Let me show you beauty. Let me give you life.*

"Get out of here, you moron!" I yelled at Stan, who was still gaping at the destruction. "Don't let the damned lab get blown up again!"

"What about you guys?" he cried. "Come on!"

I knew there was no way I could drag Ralph the twenty or so feet to the RV. If Stan tried to help us, he could get killed. I already knew that fire couldn't hurt me and Ralph, but Stan would be barbecued vampire in an instant.

"Just go! Hurry!"

The dragon issued an unearthly shriek. Twin streams of fire shot out from its nostrils and skimmed across the top of the RV.

"I'll get help!" Stan slammed the door. Seconds later the RV started up and sped out of the parking lot.

The dragon returned its attention to us; we made much easier targets. I stood up and grabbed Ralph under the arms. I dragged him toward the Honda, which wasn't exactly great protection. But there was nowhere else to hide.

I barely made it a couple of feet.

Fire engulfed us.

Chapter 14

I dropped Ralph and covered him. His body was lifeless. No breath, no heartbeat, no warmth.

Please be okay. Please be okay. Please be okay.

I squeezed my eyes shut and thought about how much I didn't want to die. And then I thought about how often my life had been in jeopardy since coming to Broken Heart.

I cracked open my eyes. The dragon's flames flowed over us. Fire tore at our clothes with hot, sharp claws. I could feel its heat, its stinging caress on my face and hands, but it didn't burn me. The flames rolled along our exposed skin with lover's fingers.

"Stop," I shouted, unsure who I was talking to. The dragon? The fire? The little voice in my head telling me I was nuts?

The fire was extinguished instantly. I could control it. Well, hell. I guess I was a dragon after all. That was the weirdest thing that had ever happened to me, and that was saying a lot.

I crawled off Ralph, the acrid smell of burned plastic and charred metal plugging my nose. Our clothes were singed, but otherwise okay. I could taste the soot, feel the magnetic draw of the fire. I had to resist its call.

For Ralph.

Once again, I grabbed him under the arms and heaved him toward the Honda.

With a snort of its nostrils, the dragon turned the soccer field behind us into a lake of fire. How much longer would we survive? Panic squeezed me, but I refused to give in to it.

I got Ralph to the car. My hands were shaking and my head was filled with the fire's song. I prayed the dragon wouldn't attack us again. We needed the car to get away. I wondered if Stan had called for help, and if so, when the hell it would get here.

The passenger door was locked.

Shit, shit, shit. Ralph had had the keys in his hand. Where were they now? I didn't have time to search the parking lot.

My mind raced. The heat of the torched car battered my back and legs. Sweat popped out of every pore. Dragonfire was damned hot. And yet, it felt so good.

I wished I had my purse, but it had never been returned. I had all kinds of useful tools inside it, including just the item I needed to unlock the passenger door. Instead, I took off my coat, wrapped a sleeve around my hand, and punched the edge of the window. Tempered glass never shattered when hit in the middle, but the edges were weaker. My dad had taught me that.

I unlocked the door and kneeled on the driver's seat, leaning over to take Ralph under the arms and pull him into the car. I got him settled and strapped on the seat belt. I sat down, heart pounding.

Why hadn't the dragon attacked again? It was only a matter of time.

Ralph was still unconscious. At least I hoped he was only unconscious. Weren't vampires supposed to be fast healers? Not to mention he had an affinity for dragonfire, too. If it didn't hurt me, then it shouldn't hurt him.

My dad had also taught me how to hotwire a car. Luckily, the Honda was an older model, so it was easy to pluck out the needed wires.

The engine turned over. Yes!

Something rapped on my window.

"Aaaaaaahhhhh!" My heart nearly stuttered out of my chest. The fire song was menacing now; its perilous tones made my hair stand on end. I didn't want to look, but I did anyway.

The man standing next to the car was more than six feet tall and built like a linebacker. His eyes were completely black. His clothing was odd; the iridescent material gleamed like a million jewels. The color was very similar to . . . oh, crap. He wasn't wearing clothes. Those were scales.

He was the dragon. The one who'd killed the woman at the cemetery.

"I will only tell you once," he said in a gravelly voice. "Get out."

I nodded and smiled and revved the gas, my hand on the gear shift. I looked behind me and whipped the Honda into reverse, pressing the gas hard. The tires spun as the car fishtailed wildly.

If this had been a movie, I would've expertly whipped the car around and sped away. Instead, I went twenty miles an hour, the car weaving. I had forgotten to turn on the lights, but I didn't want to try and risk wrecking us.

I stared over my shoulder, trying to maneuver toward the exit, when I heard a big *whump*. The front of the car dipped. Startled, I turned around and saw the man crouched on the hood.

He placed his palms on the car. Purplish blue light emanated from his hands.

The engine died.

"What's going on?" asked Ralph groggily.

"Something really, really bad," I said, frantically turning the wheel back and forth, my foot pressing the pedal to the floor. The car didn't budge.

I saw Ralph's eyes widen. "Get out," he yelled, echoing the demands of the dragon. He wrestled with the seat belt, but I knew it was too late.

"Can't you hear the song?" I whispered. Our death dirge was woven inside it.

Gripping the steering wheel so hard my fingers hurt, I sucked in a shaky breath. Fear jitterbugged through me.

The dragon walked to the passenger side. He leaned in through the broken window, his empty gaze on mine. "I don't repeat myself."

He ripped off the door and flung it over the car. It scudded across the parking lot. Vaguely, I noticed the red dragon still circling above us.

"What do you want?" I asked.

"You."

"Leave her alone!" Ralph tried to push him away, but the guy didn't move.

He grabbed Ralph by the shoulders and ripped him out of the car, seat belt and all.

"Ralph!" It took precious seconds to get out of my seat belt. I stumbled out of the car and rounded it, not sure what I planned to do.

The dragon flung his magic at me and, suddenly, it was as if I was welded to the ground. I couldn't move my feet.

Helpless and frustrated, I watched as he threw Ralph to the ground and banged his head again and again against the blacktop. The fifth time his skull bounced off the parking lot, he passed out.

"Ralph!" I looked at the dragon, my eyes hot with tears. "Don't hurt him, please."

"Give me your power now or I will remove his head."

"I don't know what you're talking about!"

"My sister gave you her dragon soul. You have all her power. And, it appears, her morality." He chuckled. "Give me her power and I promise your deaths will be quick."

"That's quite the bargain," I said. "But I can't give you my power." I really couldn't. I didn't know how to do it. His sister had kissed me, and I sure as heck wasn't about to kiss him.

His smile revealed double rows of needle-sharp teeth. *The better to eat you with, my dear.* He walked to me and grabbed my shoulder, dragging me closer and looking at me like I was crud he'd scraped off his boot. His meaty hand gripped my shoulder, and he raised his other hand. Ralph's limp body rose into the air and slowly spun in a circle.

"Give me your power, or I will kill your lover."

"I can't!" I screamed. My heart thundered in my chest, and fear squeezed my insides. I had no doubt that this dragon-man meant what he said. I'd seen this in the movies a dozen times. The bad guy got what he wanted, then killed the hapless victims anyway. Our lives were forfeit. I couldn't help but think of his twin sons, who'd already lost their mother.

"I'll give you my power," I said, "if you promise to let Ralph live."

His answer to my request was to drop Ralph onto the pavement.

"Libby?" Ralph was awake. He rolled onto his side, his gaze lifting to mine.

"It's okay," I said. "It's okay."

Then Ralph lifted his hands and fire shot from his palms. The flames wrapped around the dragon's head. He was more startled than harmed by the action, but he let me go. I scrambled toward Ralph, who got to his feet, keeping his fire aimed at the dragon. I stood behind him, feeling helpless.

"Vampire fire is weak," said the dragon-man. "Would you like to see real power?"

He lifted his hands, and I knew we were gonna die.

Take Ralph's fire, daughter. The fire wasn't just singing now. It was offering instructions. *It will protect you.*

I wrapped my arms around Ralph's midsection and listened with all my heart to the fire. Flames surrounded us. Safe. We were so safe. Our fires joined—mine orange and Ralph's red—and those strands of security wound together.

146

Light exploded around us.

I closed my eyes and pressed my cheek against Ralph's back. He held on to my quivering arms.

The heat was intense.

"No!" shouted our enemy. "No!"

I could hear the fire protesting his magic. I knew, from the wavering music, that our bubble of protection would weaken soon.

I smelled burning cotton and felt my clothes peel away from my body. I didn't want to look. Ralph and I could withstand the flames. Our clothing, however, wasn't dragon-proof.

I don't know how long I stood there waiting for our protection to dissolve and the bad guy to cut us both down.

The music changed. The menacing song of the dragon-man disappeared. I heard the triumph of our fire rise up like a choir of angels.

Then the fire was silenced.

"Libby?" Ralph's voice was hoarse.

"Yeah?"

"You okay?"

I didn't get a chance to answer. I heard shouting voices and feet scuttling on the blacktop. And then an Irish-tinged voice yelled, "Over here."

I opened my eyes, too afraid to let go of Ralph. All the fire was gone—the minivan, the soccer field, our shield, too.

Sparks floated around us like dancing fireflies. Ash filled the air like snow—our clothes.

Oh, jeez. We were practically naked.

The only clothing left between us was the piece of Ralph's shirt where my cheek had been pressed. Nearly everything else had burned away.

I peeked over Ralph's shoulder. The only thing I saw was Stan and his friend in the silver suit.

"Aw, crap," I muttered.

They aimed fire extinguishers at us and white foam spurted. The nasty chemical puffs covered us from head to toe.

Well, at least we weren't naked anymore.

Chapter 15

"No offense, Patsy," said Ralph, "but nowhere in Broken Heart is safe. Not even the mansion."

We were wrapped in blankets and sitting on the trunk of Ralph's car. I was so tired. Ralph was feeling better because a donor had arrived and let him nosh. That's why he'd been so easily knocked out—he'd been weakened by lack of blood.

I was hungry, too, and I wanted meat. I was ashamed I craved the cooked flesh of an animal, but the desire was there. Steak. Medium-rare. I was salivating at the thought.

Patsy, Gabriel, the scary green-eyed dude, and Lorcan stood in front of us. Other people ran around the area, doing what I didn't know. Nothing was salvageable here. We'd gone over what had happened a hundred times, but they kept asking questions and picked at parts of our story. I knew they were trying to find something—*anything*—that would help them prepare for the next attack.

The dragons would be back. Everyone knew it.

"This whole situation has gotten bigger than all of us," said Patsy. "But you're right, Ralph. I don't know where safe is anymore."

Ralph and I wanted to go back to his house and chill out. I wanted a shower. And I wanted to pretend to be normal for just a little while.

"Are you sure there were two dragons?" asked Patsy. Again.

I stopped short of rolling my eyes.

Ralph nodded. "We think the one who attacked was the same one from the cemetery. Did you ever find anything, Damian?"

Green Eyes shook his head. "We never found a body."

Ralph sighed. "I think the second dragon is involved with Lia."

"Great. So she's hooked up with some bad-ass dragon who wants his sister's power," said Patsy. "Let's hope Ash knows what the hell she's doing."

"She's the only one who can kill him," said Gabriel. "She's the Convocation's number one assassin. And the only one of her kind."

"And what kind is that?" I asked.

"She's a soul shifter. She absorbs the souls, and the forms, of the people she . . . er, releases from the bonds of earth," said Gabriel. "The sooner she catches her dragon, the better for us. She has to take a soul every ninety days, no matter what, or she dies."

Patsy shuddered. "Believe me, you don't want to be near her when that shit goes down."

"I think Libby should go to the hospital," said Ralph. "He banged her up pretty good."

"You, too," I said.

"Dragon or not, you both probably need to be checked out," said Patsy. "Tell you what—go to the hospital and, if Dr. Merrick gives you the thumbs-up, you can return to Ralph's house and get some rest. I'll send some guardians over there, just to be safe."

Dr. Merrick was tall, slender, and very well dressed. I could sense something otherworldly about her, but unlike every other person I'd met so far, she didn't have an aura. At least, not one I could detect.

Lucky for me and Ralph, Patsy had arranged for someone to bring us clothes. I wore the pajamas and a pair of Ralph's socks. Ralph had tucked into a shirt, jeans, and an old pair of sneakers. We both had borrowed coats draped on the table near the door.

"You and Ralph are fine. Well, he's still dead."

"Ha ha, doc," said Ralph.

She smiled. "No internal bleeding, broken bones, or other trauma I could find. If you experience pain, nausea, headaches, or double vision, come back so I can check you out again."

With that prognosis, she left. Ralph and I looked at each other. It felt awkward between us, the way it always did without the fire. I wondered if the doctor counted heartache among the symptoms that would get me a recheck. Probably not. That pain was my own, and I wasn't sharing it.

"Let's go," said Ralph.

We left the exam room and walked down the hallway. The hospital was small, but obviously well funded. New building or not, it had that cloying antiseptic smell found in every hospital.

The sparkly tattooed lady . . . Brigid, right? Yeah. She stood in the hallway, but had obviously just stepped out from a patient's room.

"Brigid," said Ralph. "How are they?"

Her smile was warm, even though her eyes held resignation. "It's a terrible thing," she said in her Irish lilt, "to have the power of gods, and not be able to save me own grandson." Her gaze darted toward the opened door.

My heart dropped to my toes. I didn't want to see what I had done. On purpose or not, I'd hurt someone, someone who might not live because of my actions.

Ralph took my hand, and I was grateful for his

intuitive, silent support. Brigid gestured toward the room and, reluctantly, I peeked inside.

Two hospital beds had been pushed together. Patrick and his wife lay shoulder to shoulder with the thin white covers pulled up to their chins. I noticed Patrick's hair was black again. Both were ghastly pale, and it didn't take a doctor to know that they weren't doing well.

Each had an IV hooked up to their arms. The thin plastic tubes delivered blood. Uncomfortable, I stepped back.

"We keep hoping fresh blood will revive them," said Brigid. "We've tried every kind: donors, Ancients, lycans, even mine."

"If you're a goddess, why can't you fix them?" I asked. I wasn't even sure I believed she was a goddess.

"There are rules," she said vaguely.

"Libby Monroe?" said a woman's voice.

Ralph and I turned around. The woman was tall and lithe, her long black hair worn plaited. She was dressed in tight black jeans, a pink leather jacket, and some kick-ass boots. She also wore a white David and Goliath T-shirt that said, "Boys are stupid, throw rocks at them!"

The most intriguing thing about her was her eyes. They were so gray they looked nearly translucent. It was creepy, her stare. Power emanated from her; she had a caged strength that I didn't want to see unleashed. Her outline was a rainbow of shifting colors. I was amazed by her aura, since every other person I'd met, except for the doctor, had one single color.

She tilted her head at me. "Damn it. He got Sybina. Why the hell did she give *you* her soul?"

"What?" I gaped at her. *"What?"*

"Who's Sybina?" asked Ralph.

"Perhaps you should start from the beginning, Ash," said Brigid in her soothing way.

Ash was staring at Ralph. "You have some of Sybina's energy, too. It's like her soul was split in half."

"That's not exactly the beginning," said Brigid.

Ash looked from Brigid to Ralph and me. "Oh, right. I'm Ash and I've come to slay the dragon."

Ralph and I took a hurried step back. Ralph hit the wall and I smacked into Brigid.

"Oh, please. You're not *really* dragons. A dragon is born, not made. You have Sybina's magic and her fire, but your human sides dampen them. And since you split her energy, it's less potent. It's not like you're going to go all scaly and sprout wings."

"That's a relief," I said, not really feeling relieved. "If you're not . . . uh, slaying us, why are you here?"

"Patsy and Gabriel gave me the four-one-one," said Ash. "I just wanted to get a firsthand account. But now I know the ending of the story. Sybina gave you her soul."

"And you wanted it," said Brigid.

"She was gifting me with it," said Ash. "We had a deal. But her brother Synd wanted it, too."

"Well, you can have it," I said. "How do I give it back to you?"

"If I sucked your soul out of your body," she said, "you'd be mine forever. All of you, and not just the part of Sybina you carry within you."

"Oh." I swallowed the knot in my throat. Sheesh. This chick was more than a little scary. "Then I guess I'll just keep it."

"I've lived a long time in this world, and even I know little about dragons," said Brigid, her gaze on Ash. "But you do."

"Yeah. I'm a compendium of useless dragon facts. Fat lot of good it does me. I'm headed back to the mansion. I gotta put my two cents in on the battle plans."

Battle plans? Oh, shit. The vampires were going to war with Synd . . . and PRIS was on its way to make things much, much worse. What the hell had I been thinking?

"Wait," said Brigid. "Can vampires be poisoned by dragons?"

Ash's eyebrows rose, and her expression was filled with disbelief. "Oh, c'mon. Don't tell me some schmuck got the bright idea of sucking dragon's blood?"

I flinched. "Schmuck is kinda harsh."

Her gaze was scathing. "You did it? I guess you have more dragon magic than I thought. Lucky it's an easy fix. Gotta make a potion with dragon saliva, fairy sparkles, and a shot of bourbon."

"What's the bourbon for?" I asked.

"To get the taste of dragon spit out of your mouth."

Brigid called Dr. Merrick, who arrived a few minutes later. Ash told her what was needed, and she gave Ash an assessing look. "I've never heard of this cure."

"You ever had a patient suffering from dragon poisoning?"

"Point taken." Dr. Merrick led the way into the room. A nurse arrived with specimen cups and a fifth of bourbon.

"Is whiskey medicinal?" I asked, amazed that they'd found alcohol so quickly.

"I believe in being prepared," said Dr. Merrick primly. She handed me a specimen cup. "Spit."

"Ew. Why can't Ralph spit?"

"Both of you spit," said Ash. "Better chance of this working. Where are the sparkles?"

"Here." Brigid lifted her hand over an empty cup and sparkling gold flakes fell into it.

Ralph spit first, which was not sexy at all, thank you. I added my saliva to his and handed the cup to Dr. Merrick. She mixed everything together.

"Is this enough?" asked Dr. Merrick, looking at the slimy gold concoction. She sounded doubtful.

"Shouldn't take that much," said Ash. "The fairy sparkles increase the potency. Throw in the bourbon and get some straws."

"Patrick and Jessica are comatose, so we'll have to forego the straws." Dr. Merrick poured in the bourbon and stirred. She glanced at the nurse. "I need a 3 ml syringe."

I couldn't watch the doctor shoot that gnarly drink in the vampires' mouths. I turned away and stared at the blank wall. Ralph didn't have a problem watching, but he did take my hand and squeeze. Man, he was really good at that comfort thing.

"How long does it take to work?" asked Brigid. Her voice held hope and excitement.

"Should be quick," answered Ash. "Like I said, the fairy sparkles amp up its power."

We waited. And waited. I got tired of staring at the wall and turned around. Patrick and Jessica didn't look any better. Their outlines were both a fading blue. I didn't want to say anything, but I knew the cure hadn't worked.

Everyone turned their gazes to Dr. Merrick. She shook her head slightly. Brigid sank into a chair near the bed, her sad gaze on her grandson.

"Shit," said Ash. "Looks like Libby was dragon

enough to poison him, but not dragon enough to cure him."

"How do you know it's the spittle that's not working?" asked Dr. Merrick.

"Seriously?" Ash rolled her eyes like that was the dumbest question she'd ever heard.

"Wait a minute. If our saliva isn't strong enough to rid Patrick of the poison, then . . . " He trailed off, his gaze on mine.

"Yep," said Ash. "We need a loogie from a real dragon."

Chapter 16

Getting dragon spit was not something arranged easily. Ash agreed to bring up the saliva issue at Patsy's meeting of the undead minds.

Since we had not been invited to the big war-planning party, Ralph and I got into his beat-up Honda and went to his house. I was so tired. My muscles ached and my head throbbed.

I was a dragon.

I held within me the soul of a creature so rare that not even a goddess knew much about it.

With these thoughts circling, I followed Ralph into his home. I felt the cold concrete even through the thick socks. Good thing it hadn't snowed, though I could still feel that possibility in the whipping wind. I had no idea what I was going to do about shoes and clothes. I had bigger worries, though. Dragon attacks. PRIS rescue. Missing parents.

Ralph flipped on the lights. "I'll shower first. While you're taking one, I'll make you something to eat."

"Okeydokey." I yawned as I took off my coat and hung it on the hall tree in the foyer. When I looked at Ralph, I saw his eyes on my breasts, which were trying to pop out of the buttoned pajama top. My nipples were saying hello, mainly because it was so chilly in the house. But then they tightened and tingled because of Ralph's attention.

"I'll . . . uh, go take that shower now." Ralph turned and hurried down the hall.

I wasn't sure if I felt complimented or insulted.

I don't know what little devil made me follow him. But I was surprised when Ralph headed toward the toddlers' bedroom. He flicked on the light and went to sit on the bed nearest the door. He picked up the teddy bear and stroked its tiny head.

I tiptoed to the doorway and peeked around the frame to watch him. He was in so much pain. I felt badly for him, for all the vampire parents. Raising children was difficult enough when you were alive. I couldn't imagine how hard it was if you were undead.

"Sometimes," he said, looking up at me (I really should work on being more sneaky), "I think it would be best if the boys lived with their grandparents. If they lived with Maura and Harold, they'd have a more normal life—one lived in the sun. And they'd have everything they could ever want."

"Money doesn't buy love," I said softly. "And no amount of trinkets could replace you, Ralph. You're their father."

"Yeah," he said. "I miss them. I think it's time they came home."

He stood up and, for a moment, we just looked at each other. Then he broke eye contact, and whatever moment had been building between us was broken.

Ralph went to take his shower, and I went to the kitchen. I sat at the table, laying my head on its smooth surface. I'd barely closed my eyes when I felt Ralph tap my shoulder.

"That was fast," I said, scooting away from the table.

"I also hold the world speed record for showering." He grinned at me and winked. Oompa! Sexy, sexy man. It didn't help that he'd only slipped on a pair of pajama bottoms. Yowzer. I really wanted to run my fingers through the damp curls on his chest.

"Toast okay?"

I pried my gaze off his pectorals. "I'd eat a cooked floor tile at this point."

He laughed, and I went to the bathroom before I did something stupid, like toss Ralph to the floor and ride him like my new pony.

I didn't want to think about sex, so I thought

about food. Toast wasn't all that appealing. I still craved meat and now I knew why. The dragon part of me was a carnivore. Would it be satisfied with a vegan lifestyle? I doubted it.

In the bathroom, I started the shower and shed my clothes. God, the water felt so good. I put my palms against the wall and leaned into the spray, letting the near scalding liquid pour over me. I wished it could drain away my betrayal as easily. I needed to tell Ralph what I'd done. Or maybe I should try to sneak in another phone call. Tell Brady to back off.

But what about Mom and Dad?

I felt like something was wrong, but not that they were dead. No. I would know that. They might be stuck in some hole somewhere. Maybe even hurt.

Ralph knocked on the door. "Hey, Libby?"

I turned off the water and peeked around the shower curtain. "Yeah?"

"Patsy called. She said you got a text message from your dad."

So Patsy was the one holding on to my phone. I missed having my purse. It was like living without one of my arms. "What did it say?"

"Mom says hi. Call soon, pumpkin."

Was it Dad? Or Brady pretending to be my father? Did it matter? Either way the message meant the same thing: My parents were okay. Oh, God. I nearly slid to the floor I was so relieved. "That's great. Do you think I can call my parents later?"

"Maybe." He paused, and I thought he'd walked away. Then he shouted, "Shit! The toast's burning."

I laughed as I got out of the shower and grabbed the towel Ralph had left for me. I had plenty of time to make a phone call and stop PRIS from showing up in Broken Heart. I had no idea what my parents had been doing for the last two days, but they'd obviously made it out of town without detection. It probably helped that Patsy and everyone else had been distracted.

I toweled off and redressed in my pajamas. When I opened the bathroom door, I could smell the charred bread. I hurried to the kitchen and found Ralph throwing away the toaster.

"Damned thing never worked right, but Therese would never let me get rid of it."

"Wedding present?"

He nodded, then he turned toward the counter. I suppose it was easier to get rid of the bedroom furniture, to rid himself of things that held her fragrance, her touch, her memory. But the toaster . . . he hadn't been able to let go of it. Because she'd wanted to keep it.

"Tell me about Therese."

Ralph turned and looked at me questioningly; a slice of half-buttered bread was in his hand. "Really?"

I nodded. "What was she like?"

"We met in Vegas in 2003. I was attending a bachelor party, and she was there because her parents were sponsoring some sort of museum opening in the Bellagio.

"I was enamored. She was so beautiful, and she had this wonderful laugh. She was the one who taught me to never make assumptions about people. She was raised in a family that worshipped money, but she never did." He shook his head, smiling. "Her parents never thought I was good enough for her, but they sure warmed up after the twins were born."

"Why did you come to Broken Heart?" I asked. "Why come to Oklahoma at all?"

"This house. We grew up here, but after my parents died, my sister and I went to live with our aunt and uncle in Tulsa. My sister lived here a while, but got married herself and moved to Missouri. Therese fell in love with the place."

No, she'd fallen in love with Ralph and realized how uncomfortable he would've been in her world. So she'd settled into his. I liked her, this woman who'd found joy with the man who loved her, and not with what he could give her.

"The happiest times of my life were with her," said Ralph. "When she died, it felt like part of me had died, too. But I had the boys. I had to be there for them."

He stared at the floor, and I stayed quiet. I had seen my parents in this type of marital ritual. Dad was the listener, my mother the talker. Even so, I understood now those long silences during their conversations. It wasn't really silence, it was patience and love. I think love involved a lot of waiting—waiting for your partner to talk or to kiss you or to come home.

And so I waited.

He sighed, and I knew he felt the weight of the world on his shoulders. "We had such a short amount of time together. She died in 2006. Michael and Stephen had just turned a year old. I talk about her to the boys all the time. I don't want them to forget her."

If I wasn't already head over heels for Ralph, I would've tipped over the edge right then. Yeah, yeah, I know. He was the Chachi to my Joanie, okay?

"Are you going to get the twins and bring them home? I haven't played Chutes and Ladders in a long time."

He chuckled. "They're a little too young for that one. When they do come home, how about a rousing game of Blue's Clues?"

"Deal."

It seemed kind of silly to make those promises. We didn't know what life was going to be like. I had no intention of living in Broken Heart. I mean, why would I? My heart stuttered. The *numero uno* reason stood near the counter buttering bread for toast I wasn't gonna eat.

I crossed the kitchen, and Ralph dropped the bread. His gaze was on mine. I wanted him, and he wanted me. There was no fire working mojo on our emotions. It was just us. I took Ralph's hands, which were rough and calloused. Working man's hands. I kissed each knuckle. Then I opened his fingers up and turned his hands over. I pressed my lips to the center of each palm.

Wordlessly, Ralph led me into his bedroom and shut the door behind him. A single lamp barely penetrated the darkness of the room. But I didn't need to see everything. Just him.

Before I knew it, we'd tumbled onto the bed. He rolled me into his arms and looked down at me.

"You really are special to me, Libby." Ralph cradled my face.

"I'm feeling mushy about you, too," I said. Oh yeah, I was definitely having a mondo attack of the warm fuzzies.

I dared to slip inside his pajama bottoms and was rewarded with his bare buttocks. I cupped his tight ass, and he groaned, rubbing his cock against me.

"We can't," he whispered, unbuttoning my top. "We can't."

"We can." I pried one of my hands between us and dipped inside the silky pants to touch his shaft.

He felt velvet-smooth, and hard. I had never had the pleasure of touching a man's penis before. I was nearly delirious with the idea of what he would feel like inside me.

Ralph's lips discovered my breasts. He laved one nipple into hardness, and then suckled it. Sensations rolled through me, a thousand fabulous zips and zaps. His lips clamped around my other nipple, while his fingers rolled the wet peak.

Oh! Oh! Oh yeah!

I pushed off his pants and tried to wiggle out of mine, but then Ralph did something really moronic.

He scuttled away from me. "Stop, Libby. Please."

"No way." I got rid of my pajama bottoms and straddled him.

His gaze was drawn to my nudity, especially the part between my legs. He couldn't seem to stop himself from touching my curls.

His finger stroked my clit.

"Ralph!" I nearly swallowed my tongue.

He snatched his hand away. "Really. Libby. I mean it."

"Uh-huh." I rolled his pants down and rubbed my wet heat against his cock. Sparks of pleasure shot into my womb. "It's never been like this for me. Can't we finish?"

His hands clamped my hips, forcing me to stop. I looked at him, my heart thudding. His expression was pure torment.

"You don't understand," said Ralph. "If we make love, we'll be bound."

"Okay." I twitched my hips.

He groaned, his eyes closing briefly. "For a hundred years."

"Sounds good." I held on to his hands and leaned forward. "Now, let's go."

"Oh, God." He gritted his teeth, and once again stalled my movements. "Libby, if we make love, we'll be married. For a hundred years."

His tone got through the haze of my lust before his words did. I worried my lower lip as I thought about what he said. "You mean, if we have sex, we're mated?"

Hadn't Stanley said that Patrick and Jessica were bound? The fate of one depended on the fate of the other. If Patrick died, so would she. That was a tad more commitment than a plain ol' human marriage.

I sighed woefully. "I suppose it's too early in the relationship to get hitched for a century."

"Hey, now. We could . . . " He trailed off, and I looked at him, hope renewed. He shook his head. "This is all happening too fast."

I wasn't a hussy, although I really wanted to be *his* hussy. His reluctance, however justified, was putting a dent in my self-esteem.

"No one's wanted me before, and you do," I said, as if offering my virginity would persuade him to rock my world.

"No one's wanted you?" He gently lifted me off and slid out from underneath me. "I've wanted you since the second I met you."

I noticed Ralph's fangs were extended. Stimulating a vampire's hunger could be a dangerous thing. I put a hand to my throat and gulped.

"I want to make love to you," said Ralph, "even though we can't completely bind."

"Okay," I said, lust blooming in my core. "Okay."

Ralph's gaze slid over every inch of my skin. I returned the favor. He was lean and muscled, with curly brown hair on his chest and legs. I gripped his shaft, my fingers stroking the velvety skin.

He groaned, his hand stalling mine. "It's been a long time. We better go slow."

I released him, unsure of what to do next. I needn't have worried. Ralph knew exactly what to do.

"You're so beautiful," he murmured. "Let me touch you."

Ralph's fingers danced on my bare skin. He left no place unexplored, and every feathery touch made me want more.

He skimmed the underside of my breasts, teasing my areolae. He suckled one nipple, letting go to blow softly on the crinkled flesh until the peak tightened even more. He did the same to my other nipple. Sensations rippled and my belly quivered.

Desire liquefied me. I stroked his rib cage, my fingers running through the hair on his chest. Then I found *his* nipples. I rubbed them to hardness, then lightly twisted.

Ralph sucked in a sharp breath.

"Oops." I did it again.

With lips and hands and words, he worshipped me. I felt like a goddess, and he was my supplicant.

I melted under his gentleness. I tried to make him feel the same, but I'd never been with a man. I wasn't naive, but nervous . . . yeah, I was definitely nervous. My whole body quaked, but Ralph soothed every tremor.

He was patient. He knew how to build the fires, and he was good at it, too. Wow. I'd never felt this way about a man. I had never really felt the tender temptation of lust, of such terrible need. But what unfolded inside me, other than lust, was the absolute knowledge that Ralph was the *one*. I didn't care if we could never consummate our relationship, or that he was an immortal vampire. I would give myself to him, heart and soul.

I doubted much in my life. I questioned everything because I had been taught to do so. The establishment said that love built slowly. That people had to court each other, and withstand rituals and relationship milestones to earn the right to love. They had to marry, have kids, contribute to society.

God, what a terrifyingly boring way to fall in love.

I was already on the precipice, and I didn't fall off the cliff.

I jumped.

Ralph cupped my sex and caressed the outer lips. He pierced me with one finger, and I sucked in a breath. "Oh."

He kissed me lazily as he moved a second finger inside. Then he stroked in and out in a rhythm that made me ever so happy.

Ralph covered me, sliding his cock against my clit. I was so wet for him, so ready for him to take me. I moaned, my hips matching his rhythm.

My restless hands fluttered to his shoulders, my nails digging into his skin as he rubbed his shaft faster and faster against me.

My legs trembled and my heart thudded as he brought me closer and closer to ecstasy. I wrapped my legs around his buttocks and clawed at his flesh, my moans and movements just as frantic as his.

Our eyes met, and that was it, I flew over the edge into bliss.

Seconds later, I heard Ralph's groan. His cock trembled against me as he came, his hot seed spilling onto my stomach.

He lay on top of me and looked into my eyes, smiling. "You have my heart," he whispered.

"And you have mine."

Dragonfire exploded around us. I heard its song,

which trilled about love and connection. About two souls joined as one.

"Um, Libby?"

"Yes, Ralph?" I reveled in our flames of l-o-v-e. We were meant for each other. We were literally hot for one another. We were burning for—

"Sweetheart," said Ralph, his voice snapping me out my lovey-dovey thoughts. "The bed's on fire."

Chapter 17

I yelped, and Ralph fell off me, his hand pressing against his right pectoral.

Above my right breast, it felt as though a poker had been jabbed into my skin. It was so hot and painful that it brought tears to my eyes.

The fire itself didn't harm us. The bed covers and furniture weren't so lucky. Holy shit! I sat up and patted the covers, which only made it worse. My dragonfire kept adding fuel to the flames.

Ralph leapt from the bed and ran out of the bedroom, only to return with a fire extinguisher.

He aimed and white foam exploded.

"Goddamn it!" I shouted. "I'm so sick of this stuff."

"Sorry, honey," said Ralph. He put down the extinguisher. He was trying really hard not to laugh.

"It's not funny." I wiped off my chest. I blinked down at the spot above my right breast. "What's that?"

"I have one, too."

On both of our chests was the same mark: A circle about the size of a quarter with two slanted black lines through its middle.

Ralph looked at me. "What just happened?"

"I . . . I don't know." I looked at my mark, then at his. I was flabbergasted. "Is it a vampire thing?"

"No. When we claim others, we leave our marks on them, but they can only be seen by other vampires. This is like a tattoo."

"Do you think it's dragon-related?"

"Probably," he said. "I wonder what it means."

"I don't want to know."

Ralph walked to the bed and sat down, right in the white fluff. I loved him for that. He wound his fingers through mine. "Hey, now. Don't look like that. We'll figure it all out."

"Really?"

"Of course." He sat up and drew me with him. "Let's get cleaned up."

We took a shower together. Ralph washed my hair, and I washed his. Then we kissed a lot and, after a while, the water turned cold. But steam still rose from our dragon-heated bodies.

"Damn. No towels," said Ralph. "I'll go get a couple from the dryer."

"What about clothes?" I asked. "I think mine went up in the bed fire."

"I'll rustle you up something."

He turned around and opened the door. His ass looked so cute, I reached out and pinched one taut cheek. He laughed as he stepped into the hallway. I was behind him, my hands reaching toward his buttocks for one more squeeze.

He stopped suddenly and I rammed into him.

"Hey!" I wrapped my arms around his waist and let my hands wander south.

"Libby," he said. There was warning in his tone, but I didn't understand why.

"My God, Randolph, who *is* this person?"

The cultured voice was female, her tone designed to freeze the unworthy. I let go of Ralph and backed away. Oh, my God! Who was that?

"If you don't mind, Maura, I'd like to get dressed."

"We'll meet you in the living room," she said stiffly.

Ralph turned around. "I'll bring you something to wear."

"Okay." I looked at his closed expression. "Who was that?"

"My mother-in-law."

* * *

Ralph's mother-in-law sat on the couch, waiting for us like a principal getting ready to dress down the naughty students.

Dressed in a pair of Ralph's sweats and an old T-shirt, I settled into a recliner near the TV. Ralph chose to stand, arms crossed, his gaze narrowed.

The woman's silver hair was coiffed in an updo, her brown eyes as hard and flat as pebbles. She was dressed in a Donna Karan pantsuit and she practically dripped with diamonds. Her mink coat was folded on the arm of the couch.

"This is Maura Brighton," said Ralph. "Therese's mother. Where's Harold? Where are the boys? Are they okay?"

"Everyone's perfectly fine."

"What are you doing here?"

"I could ask the same of you, Randolph. What are you doing here?"

"I've only been back a day," Ralph lied smoothly. "And it was unexpected. I planned to call you tomorrow."

"Is she your housekeeper?" the woman asked, her gaze bouncing around the room, as if to say, *She doesn't do a good job, does she, darling?* Yeah, right. She knew I wasn't a housekeeper, especially since I was just naked in the bathroom with him. If she meant to insult me, she didn't come close. I'd been called a lot worse names by a lot better people. After all, I was the daughter of the nation's best-known kooks.

"Her name is Libby Monroe. She's very special to me."

Maura's china-doll features mottled. "You're *dating*? My daughter is barely in the grave, and you're already trying to replace her?"

"Therese died two years ago," said Ralph patiently. I'd bet everything in my bank account Ralph hadn't dated, much less been in a serious relationship, since his wife passed.

She sniffed as her gaze once again found her surroundings lacking. She looked at me and smiled coldly. "You're not nearly as pretty as she was."

"Probably not," I said easily. "I bet she was beautiful. And I think she was very special."

Maura looked thunderstruck. It was obvious that relations between Ralph and his in-laws were strained enough without adding me into the mix. I'm sure she didn't expect kindness from someone she viewed as her daughter's replacement.

"You didn't answer my question about the boys," said Ralph. "Where are they?"

Maura's expression soured. "They're in the car with Harold."

Ralph left the room. When he returned, two blond-haired tykes were squealing in his buff arms. Ralph the Daddy was the sexiest thing I'd ever seen.

He kissed them, tickled them, and hugged them. I'd never seen a man more happy. Ralph needed to be with his sons. They were a family. I couldn't deny I yearned to be part of it.

Another man entered the living room, looking as dour as Maura. He joined his wife on the couch. He was dressed in Armani, folding his coat into a square on his lap. His eyes were also brown, and less warm than his wife's.

"Teddy missed you guys," said Ralph. "You wanna go say hi?"

"Teddy!" shouted the munchkins.

Ralph made airplane noises and tucked one boy under each arm. He flew them into their room. I studied the carpet while Ralph got his sons settled. I bet he wasn't going to let them go. Not ever again.

Minutes later, Ralph returned, and he looked really pissed. I didn't blame him.

"You showed up in the middle of the night and snuck into my home. Why?"

"We were hardly sneaking. We have a key. Honestly, Randolph. Why didn't you tell us you'd returned from Saudi Arabia?" accused Maura, who apparently was the mouthpiece for her and her husband. Her frosty gaze slid over me. Whatever, lady.

Ralph's eyes went red; he stared at Maura and Harold. In his come-hither voice, he said, "Why did you come here?"

"To pack the boys' things," said Maura woodenly.

"And to find evidence of your bad parenting," added Harold, his eyes as dazed as his wife's.

I got a perverse satisfaction out of seeing Ralph go vampire on them.

"Why?" asked Ralph.

Maura tilted her head, her empty gaze swinging to Ralph. "We're challenging you for custody of the twins."

Ralph stilled; a muscle in his jaw worked. I felt outraged on his behalf. I had no doubts that Ralph was a good father. He'd put his sons first, even if it meant sending them away.

"Your in-laws are horrid," I whispered.

"As miserable as they are, they're still my sons' grandparents. But yeah, I'm tempted to throw a fireball at them right now."

"Just one?" Yeah, yeah, bad karma. Well, I'd done plenty tonight to earn my bad karma. What was one thing more?

Amusement glimmered in his eyes. "I like your style, Libby."

He focused on them both and said, "You will both get into your car and return to your hotel in Tulsa. You'll sleep restfully, and when you awake you will only remember you took the boys home. You were happy to see them reunited with their father. Do you understand?"

"Yes," they both answered.

They stood and put on their coats. Then they walked robotlike to the front door and let themselves out. We followed them to the porch and watched. Fat snowflakes were drifting from the night sky. The ground was already blanketed in white.

We heard a car start and a sleek red Jaguar slid past the house. Good. The in-laws were leaving and I was glad to see them go.

"If Broken Heart is so protected," I asked, "how did they get in here?"

"I claimed my sons, so their marks get them a free pass. But the guardians know them, too." He turned away, and I didn't need a compass to know the direction of our relationship. I could feel the distance growing between us. I followed Ralph into the hallway. We could hear the boys in their room playing with their toys.

"Michael and Stephen being here changes everything, doesn't it?" I asked.

"Of course it does. They already have to deal with an undead father, and now I'm a dragon, too? It's all too much."

He looked at me, his eyes filled with regret. Oh, I got it. Throwing a possible dragon girlfriend at them was the "too much" part. "They come first."

"They should," I said softly. I stopped short of saying I understood his decision. I wanted him to say that I was worthwhile, too. Why couldn't he be a father and be my lover? Well, I wasn't Therese. I could never take her place . . . not for those little boys, and not for Ralph.

But I didn't want to be a replacement, anyway.

He rubbed a hand through his hair. "It's getting close to dawn. I need to see if their nanny is available. It'll take a while to get them on a night schedule again. But Mera usually hangs during the day in case they wake up."

"I can watch them," I said. The words just popped out of my mouth. We both looked startled. "Well, I have to stay here, don't I? What were the plans for keeping me here while you zonked out?"

"We have guardians outside the house, remember?" He sighed, his gaze sliding away from mine. "I appreciate the offer, Libby, but I better call Mera. The boys know her."

"So I'm good enough to sleep with but not good enough to babysit your sons?" It was a low blow and I knew it, but it was also how I felt. I wanted him to trust me, and it hurt that he didn't.

"That's not fair, Libby. You know damned well we have something amazing together."

"Only I can't compartmentalize. I can't separate you from the other parts of my life. I'm all in, Ralph. Everything, and everyone, that comes with you."

"Are you, Libby?" He shook his head. "If you could leave Broken Heart right now, you would. You're only here because you don't have a choice."

"You're right. I'm only in Broken Heart because I don't have a choice," I said. I would not cry, damn it. "I'm standing here, with you, because I want to. That's a choice."

He opened his mouth to respond, but I held up my hand. I'd had enough drama. Everything was mixed-up and crazy. I'd come to Broken Heart to investigate reports of paranormal activity. Instead, I'd become a dragon and fallen in love with a vampire.

"Just call the nanny," I said wearily. "Do you want the couch?"

"No. I have to sleep in the bedroom. It's been sun-proofed. I have a sleeping bag that will do until I can get the bed replaced."

"Okay. Do you have extra pillows and blankets?"

"Yeah."

"Daddy! Daddy!" Michael and Stephen ran into the hallway. Ralph had already tucked them into footie pajamas with the familiar theme of trains.

Ralph bent down and scooped up his boys. "Michael. Stephen. Say hello to Libby."

"Ibby!" shouted Michael, clapping his hands. "Ibby! Ibby! Ibby!"

Stephen considered me thoughtfully, his bow-shaped lips pursed. Then he waved at me with one tiny hand. They were so cute.

"Hi," I said. "What kind of monkeys are you?" Then I tickled their ribs. They giggled and writhed.

"Whoa," said Ralph, trying to juggle them both. He gave each boy a sloppy kiss.

"Story!" yelled Michael. "Read story!"

As a child, my favorite nightly tale had been *Goodnight Moon* by Margaret Wise Brown. Surprisingly, my parents had chosen traditional bedtime stories. It was the bed that was untraditional . . . usually the pull-out in an RV or a cot in a hotel.

"Goodnight room, goodnight moon, goodnight cow jumping over the moon," I quoted.

"Goodnight wight," said Stephen in a serious little voice. "And red bawoon."

"That's right," said Ralph. He looked both surprised and pleased. "You know *Goodnight Moon*?"

"I was a kid once," I said. "And yeah, that was my favorite book."

"Theirs, too." He seemed to realize he'd been gazing tenderly at me. He cleared his throat and looked away. "C'mon, kiddos. Time to brush your teeth, and then we'll read a story."

"No brush teeth," said Michael, pouting. His brother mirrored the expression, crossing his arms and shaking his head.

"Here we go," said Ralph, chuckling. He glanced at me. "This might take a while."

I took the hint. Ralph wanted to spend time with his sons, and I wasn't part of that routine. I probably never would be. I wanted the whole package, and if Ralph wasn't part of the deal, then I didn't want to stay in Broken Heart any longer than I had to. Yeah, okay. Now that I was paranormal, too, it was probably smarter to stay here than to live in the human world as a half dragon, half dork.

I went into the living room and looked at the clock. After Ralph went to bed, I'd sneak a phone call. I needed to talk to Mom and call off the rescue mission.

I was glad she and Dad were okay, but I no longer wanted PRIS anywhere near Broken Heart. These people had enough problems without alerting humans to their presence. I couldn't bear the thought of Ralph and his boys facing that kind of scrutiny.

I looked through the books on the shelf in the living room, which was a mixture of children's books, legal thrillers, horror novels, and medical texts. I chose *Graverobbers Wanted (No Experience Necessary)* by Jeff Strand, then got cozy on the couch and started to read.

The book wasn't one that made you drowsy. In fact, every mundane noise took on an ominous tone. I draped myself in the throw that lay over the back of the couch. It was silly to seek protection from a mere blanket, but being covered up made me feel better.

Ack. It was so cold in the house! I looked around until I found the thermostat. It was set at sixty-eight degrees. No wonder I was freezing. I changed the gauge to seventy-two degrees. The heat kicked on.

I adjusted my position, settling deeper into the cushions.

The television blared to life.

"Aaaaaaahhhhh!" The book went flying as I leapt to my feet, my heart thundering. CNN rotated through the usual worldly horrors while I tried to figure out how the TV had turned on by itself.

"Melvin?" I asked cautiously. "Are you there?"

Chapter 18

Melvin could've been taking a nap or visiting Patsy or whispering madly in my ear. I was incapable of communicating with him. I didn't sense any ghost, attached to me or not.

After a moment, I calmed down. I picked up the book and the blanket, and then turned around. My gaze snagged on the remote control; it had been wedged between the cushions where I was sitting.

I laughed. Everything didn't have a supernatural explanation, after all. My ass had turned on the damned thing. Sighing with relief, I folded the throw and put it back.

I picked up the remote, sat on the couch, and pined for Ralph.

"In Tulsa, a rash of unexplained arson fires continues unabated. The most recent blaze happened only hours ago and took out the top three floors of the Crowne Plaza Hotel."

The picture shifted from the serious, well-coiffed newscasters to video footage of the raging fire. I couldn't hear the song of that horrifying blaze, and I was glad. It appeared I had to be within physical range to hear its music.

"Twenty-two people were injured," intoned the anchor. "Investigators say the arson fires were started on the tops of buildings. The locations seem random: an abandoned house on the north side of Tulsa, a kennel that specializes in training guard dogs, a nightclub in Brookside, and a bakery in the Woodland Hills area."

Started on the tops of buildings? Like a dragon might have lobbed a fireball at 'em? I watched the montage of images. The abandoned house was an old mansion, one of the many that had been built in Tulsa's oil boom days and fallen into disrepair. Perfect vampire hidey-hole. And the kennel? Hel-*lo*. Werewolves. The nightclub was easy, too. Any nocturnal paranormal creature could frequent it. The bakery . . . well, that one didn't make sense unless Mr. Dragon had a vendetta against cupcakes. The hotel didn't make sense, either.

I sighed and flopped against the couch. What did it matter? I sure as hell didn't want to contact the police; no one would believe it was an Honest-to-God dragon causing all the fires. Besides, if it was a paranormal problem, it seemed to me there would be a paranormal solution.

I picked up Jeff Strand's book and started reading again. It was scary, but hilarious, too. I'd never read anything like it.

"Hey," said Ralph. He wore only his pajama bottoms. He looked so sexy that I wanted to nibble on him. He glanced at the book and grinned. "Eva recommended that series to me. Never thought gore could be that funny."

He held up a pillow and blanket. I met him halfway and took the bedding. "You look tired."

"Vampires don't choose their bedtimes," he said. "Sunrise means we're literally dead to the world."

"Did you get hold of Mera?"

He shook his head. "Nah. I got a better offer." He tugged the bedding he'd just given to me out of my hands and tossed it to the couch. Then he pulled me into his embrace and brushed his lips over mine. "You still up for watching two ornery little boys?"

"Really?" I leaned back and gazed at him. "Why? Was Mera unavailable?"

"I didn't call to find out." He cupped my chin. "The boys like you. And they're pretty smart. Besides, anyone who knows *Goodnight Moon* by heart is my kinda gal."

He kissed me, then pulled back.

We stared at each other, moon-eyed, and then he

sighed. "If I don't go now, I'll pass out. I usually wake up about seven or so."

"Okay." I reluctantly stepped out of his embrace. "We'll see you tonight."

After Ralph left, I listened for the click of the closed door. Then I made up the couch and looked around for the phone. There wasn't one in the living room or the kitchen, which left the bedrooms and bathroom. Probably in Ralph's room, though I didn't remember seeing one in there. Damn it. Why didn't he have a freaking telephone?

If I couldn't call my parents, I had two choices. Let Brady arrive with lasers blazing (no, I'm not kidding), or tell Ralph the truth about why I needed his cell phone.

I was sure if I admitted my deception to Ralph, he'd take away my babysitting privileges. And probably my boinking-the-hot-vampire rights, too. Damn. The situation was my fault. But how could anyone blame me for wanting my freedom?

Reluctantly, I knocked on Ralph's door. I didn't get a response, but I opened the door anyway. "Hey, Ralph?"

My heart climbed into my throat and my stomach felt like I'd swallowed bricks. I didn't want to tell him the truth. I didn't want him to stop trusting me. I liked how he looked at me like I was the last chocolate truffle in the candy box. Like he couldn't wait to unwrap me and nibble.

He was already asleep, tucked inside a green sleeping bag. He looked so yummy. I wished I could climb inside with him and touch all his manly parts.

Instead, I looked for his cell phone. I spotted it on the nightstand. I crept around Ralph. Wow. He was so still. He really did look dead, which freaked me out. I guess that was part of the perils of dating a vampire.

I snatched the phone and flipped it open. I hesitated. What if the vampires had some way of tracking phone calls? I mean, they had all kinds of mind juju. Maybe they could pluck conversations right out of the air. I didn't want to take any chances. I plugged in Mom's and Brady's numbers and then sent a text message: *All fine in BH. Stay in TX. Will call soon.*

After it sent, I went into Ralph's inbox and deleted the outgoing message. Jeez. If I was any more paranoid, I'd wipe my fingerprints off the phone.

Not a bad idea. I used my T-shirt to rub it clean and, with it still clutched in my shirt, returned it to the nightstand. Then I crept out of the room and shut the door.

Relief slid through me. I finally felt like everything would be okay. At least for now.

* * *

The boys woke me up half past the ass-crack of dawn. Or at least it felt like that. When I actually looked at the clock, it was noon.

I rolled off the couch and sat on the floor, squinting at the two boys running from one end of the living room to the other.

I had no idea what to do. I'd never babysat anything. I'd never even had a pet. Okay. Now was not the time to panic.

"Ibby!" One boy changed direction and jumped onto my lap, throwing his tiny arms around my neck. He grabbed my ears and made my sleep-deprived head waggle. "Ibby!"

This guy was definitely Michael. Stephen stood back, his teddy clutched in one fist, and eyed us suspiciously. I opened one arm. "C'mon, kid."

He shuffled forward and sat next to me. "Cookie."

"Right. You need food."

I managed to create an edible breakfast of toast, orange juice, and dill pickles. I didn't have a lot to work with. Lunch would be better—at least I hoped so.

The care and feeding of three-year-olds was nearly as draining as battling dragons. Getting them dressed the first time worked out okay, but after a misunderstanding with a jar of grape jelly and then the unfortunate ink pen episode, their third change of clothes almost required intervention by Henry Kissinger. The little buggers were good negotiators. They talked me into three cookies each and at least two piggyback rides, and that didn't include socks. The price of putting on socks was chocolate pudding.

Once the bribes had been devoured and my back ached from romping through the house, Michael and Stephen were wired by enough sugar to launch themselves to Mars.

We played trains, read books, and colored pictures. We also built castles out of wooden blocks the twins enjoyed knocking down and stomping on like mini Godzillas.

The boys demanded baloney sandwiches for lunch. Baloney and mayonnaise were off my vegan food list. I wasn't sure baloney was any kind of meat, but it still had that meaty smell. My inner dragon whined just a little.

Chasing after rambunctious toddlers was exhausting. I had to give props to Ralph, who'd taken care of this energetic twosome for three years.

The rest of the afternoon wore on without incident except for one moment in the kitchen. An accidental sock slide across the floor resulted in a skinned knee.

The boys patted my bandaged boo-boo and told me I was very brave.

It was so easy to fall in love with them.

Around four o'clock, the boys fell asleep on the

couch watching *Max and Ruby.* I crawled into the recliner and drifted off.

A low, dark pulse of music infiltrated my consciousness. My eyes fluttered open. Michael stood on the couch, clapping his hands. Stephen was curled into a ball, hugging his teddy bear. They were both looking at the ceiling, expectant.

For a second, I didn't understand all the noise. The swelling music. The angry shouts of the guardians outside. The horrible *wump-wump* sounds shaking the house.

I shot out of the chair and scooped the twins into my arms. Stephen dropped his bear and screamed, but I couldn't stop to retrieve it. The fire song clashed and clanged, rising to a near screech. Oh, God.

Terrified, I ran into the hallway.

Michael and Stephen wailed. They sensed my fear, or maybe they sensed the dragon. I reached for the door to Ralph's bedroom.

The living room exploded.

Dragonfire roared toward us.

I shoved through the doorway and slammed it shut. My heart was trying to pound out of my chest. The boys were screaming and holding on to me for dear life.

"Ibby," sobbed Michael. "I scared."

"Me, too," cried Stephen.

I wanted nothing more than to make them feel safe again. Anger tore through my fear.

I would kill that fucking dragon myself.

"It's okay. Don't you worry," I said. "Let's wake up Daddy."

I knew we only had seconds. The guardians might be able to distract the dragon long enough for me to wake Ralph. The digital clock on the night-stand read 6:03 p.m. It wasn't sunset. Would I be able to get him to open his eyes?

I put the boys down and they sat by their father, clutching at the sleeping bag. They were still crying.

I got on the other side and patted Ralph's cheeks. "Ralph? Time to get up. Come on!"

Michael slapped his dad's forehead. "Daddy! Daddy!"

"Whoa there, buddy. Let's not bruise the man," I said grabbing his arm midslap.

Above us, the top of the house crackled and crumbled. Flakes of ceiling drifted down, the pre-lude to bigger debris. The dragon's dark chorus rose in triumph.

I'd be damned if I let the twins get even a scratch on them. What could I do? Hell, I'd hide under a blanket of asbestos if it meant warding off the im-pending flames. I'd take any kind of shield at this point, even the über-techno-whatsit that Brady and his team used. I didn't know much about his invisi-ble force-field gizmo. I was never allowed to use one. In fact, only Brady and his four team members utilized them.

A force field, invisible or not, would come in really damned handy. The house quaked and shivered, reminding me of the wood-block castles the boys had knocked down. Pictures crashed to the floor, and the dresser mirror shattered.

I got as close as I could to Ralph. I grabbed the toddlers, tucking them between us. I had never been so scared in my life. I would've given anything to make sure those boys and Ralph would be protected.

The fire will protect you, daughter. Yeah, right. So far the fire hadn't helped much at all. Still, I felt my inner dragon raise its snout. Its wings unfurled. Its fire flowed. It built inside me, burbling and rising.

The boys clung to me desperately, their sobs breaking my heart.

The far wall blew inward. The ceiling caved in. The noise drowned out our screams. Choking dust rolled through the room, getting trapped in our lungs and stinging our eyes.

The red dragon hovered above us; in the fading sunlight its scales glittered like a thousand rubies. It opened its maw and unleashed a fireball. I lifted up my hand as if doing so could protect us.

But nothing could protect us. Nothing at all.

Chapter 19

We didn't die.

Somehow, we were okay. At least I thought we were. My eyes were still squeezed shut. My heart thudded erratically. The arm I had wrapped so tightly around the boys quivered.

"Pretty," said Michael. I knew it was him because he was the brave one.

Sheesh. If a three-year-old had the courage to look up, so could I. I pried open my eyes. Whoa. We were cocooned in a bubble of undulating energy.

The fire burned everything around us. The furniture became pyres; the carpet a sacrifice to the blaze. Only the walls with their peculiar silver sheen were immune.

Michael sat on his dad's chest, his wide gaze taking in the destruction. Stephen was glued to my lap.

He ducked his head against my shoulder, crying softly.

"Ssshhh," I said. "It's okay, honey."

The red dragon's fire meshed with mine; every scorching blow strengthened the shield. I knew this because I heard the song. My fire was stronger than the dragon's.

Its song was fading, and even though I couldn't see past the black smoke, I knew it was being driven away. Frustration echoed in its fire. I hoped that meant rescue was imminent.

I hugged the boys. Then I laid a hand on Ralph's cool brow. "Ralph," I whispered.

To my shock, his eyes opened.

"What's going on?" He sat up suddenly and gathered a sniffling Stephen and Michael into his arms. His gaze widened as he glanced around. "Everything's on fire."

"Don't look at me," I said, my voice shaking with relief. "I soooo didn't do this."

The fire's harmony gave way to cacophony.

Whoomp!

Every last flame and wisp of smoke was sucked away, like a giant invisible Hoover had been turned on.

My shield disappeared instantly. Apparently it wasn't immune to the vacuum. I could still feel the heated aftermath of the conflagration.

The closed door, which had somehow escaped

the destruction, burst open. Damian and his brothers stood there, all holding fire extinguishers.

I threw up my hands and wailed, "Noooooo."

Too late. All three nozzles discharged.

When they were done blasting us, the four of us were covered in a mountain of white.

"Did you really have to keep doing that?" I asked Damian. At least I think it was Damian. It was difficult to tell which brother was which.

"A precaution." I could swear he was trying not to laugh. "We weren't sure you could control your dragonfire."

"How did you get the other flames out?"

"The magic of our resident Wiccans," said Damian. "We drove off the dragon and they worked their spells."

Wiccans. I remembered Patrick talking about them cleansing his house. This town really did have every kind of paranormal being imaginable.

"Are you okay, Libby?" asked Ralph. He hugged his sons closely, and I wrapped my arms around all of them.

"Completely freaked out, thanks. What about you?"

He kissed me. And suddenly everything was all right, even with wiggling three-year-olds protesting the squishing and lycanthrope triplets witnessing our smooch. When Ralph pulled back, he was grinning. Sunlight dappled his messed-up hair and slanted across his face.

Wait a minute. Sunlight?

He looked up, blinking at the hole above us. "I haven't seen the sun in months."

"Why aren't you a pile of ash?" I asked.

"His dragon magic," said Damian. We both looked at him and he shrugged. "We've been taking a crash course in dragonology from Ash. C'mon, Lia and her dragon aren't gone for good."

"Synd wasn't with her?" asked Ralph.

"No. He's been a little busy in Tulsa setting fires, targeting the businesses and homes of paranormal beings. Ash barely escaped the blaze at her hotel."

I remembered the CNN report about the rash of supposed arson fires; the most recent one had been at the Crowne Plaza Hotel. I frowned. "How does he know which ones aren't human?"

"We don't know," said Damian. "Just like we don't know why he's torching their places. Of course, it's obvious why he wants to kill Ash."

"Because everyone does?" I asked sweetly.

Ralph laughed, and I was glad he did. There wasn't much cause for humor. The house was in shambles. The living room was smoldering embers, same as Ralph's bedroom. It had to be difficult to see the destruction of the home where he'd spent his childhood, not to mention where he'd brought his bride and raised their sons. I felt my heart break for them.

The boys' bedroom survived, and I was grateful for that. Despite Damian's insistence that we vacate, I barreled past him and his brothers.

"They need toys," I demanded. Dutifully, Damian took a book bag from the closet and scooped up playthings.

"Get the frog and the giraffe," I said. I could only hope Stephen would accept one of the stuffed animals in lieu of his fried teddy.

One of the other brothers picked up the tiny dresser full of the twins' clothes. "Let's go," he said.

Two brothers went ahead of us. Damian followed us, carrying the bag crammed full of toys. Ralph, who'd only been wearing pajama bottoms, held Michael tightly. Stephen clung to me, wailing his unhappiness about the "stinky bubbles."

Michael thought the white foam was the greatest thing since chocolate pudding, evidenced by his attempts to stuff it into his mouth. Ralph stalled that maneuver and did the best he could to swipe the crap from his son.

I cleaned off Stephen's face, which didn't do much good since the kid kept pressing it against my froth-covered shoulder.

"Where are we going?" I asked.

"Compound," said Damian. "It's the safest place."

His brothers led us to a black Hummer parked a few feet away. Its massive engine was running. The passenger-side window dropped down, and I saw a blue-haired woman in the driver's side.

"C'mon," she yelled. "We don't have a lot of time."

One of the triplets opened the door and Ralph slid in with Michael. I handed him Stephen and put my hand on the door.

I heard music. Not just music, but the gravelly voice of Kurt Cobain singing about where bad folks go when they die. I recognized the song blasting around us: Nirvana's "Lake of Fire." I didn't have to look up to know the dragons were swooping down.

"C'mon!" yelled the driver. "Move your asses!"

My gaze met Ralph's. He reached for me, but there was no time. I would never forgive myself if something happened to Ralph or those sweet little boys.

I slammed the door shut and the Hummer's wheels spun in the snow as it took off. The triplets ran for cover, but I had nowhere to go.

Twin blasts of fire knocked me off my feet. I landed on my back, skidding across the snow. Above me, I could see the red and blue dragons circling.

Bastards.

"Oh my God!" screamed a very familiar voice. "Liberty!"

My mother and father ran across the yard toward me, completely ignoring the fact that they could be fried at any second. My heart slammed against my chest as I got up.

My inner dragon roared. There was no controlling it. Maybe it was that Sybina recognized her enemies, or that I was tired of getting blown up and knocked down.

The strains of The Doors' "Light My Fire" rumbled from my core. Flames erupted along my hands, down my arms and legs.

Mom and Dad skidded to a stop about a foot away.

"Get down!" I shouted.

Dad didn't need to be told twice. He grabbed Mom's arm and chucked her into the snow, then lay on top of her. I marched across the yard. I had no idea what to do about protecting my family.

But my dragon did.

Fire swirled around me, glittering orange and red. I felt the magic in these flames. Sybina's soul was there, too. She refused to be taken. To be destroyed.

My fire song changed to Deep Purple's "Smoke on the Water." I recognized the familiar guitar chords, but there were no words. Just the driving beat of the music.

Listening to my dragon, I lifted my arms and a big column of flames shot upward. The dragons parted and the fire blasted into the night sky, dissipating into mere wisps of black smoke.

Son of a bitch. I'd missed them. *Both* of them. So much for the paranormal power of friggin' dragon-fire. I lifted my arms to gather the fire again, but it wouldn't . . . well, gather. No amount of mental cajoling helped, either. If I had known that I'd only get one chance to use my mojo, I might've aimed better. Oh, who am I kidding? I couldn't hit the broad side of a barn, much less the leathery flank of a dragon.

The red dragon broke pattern and blew fire at a circle of women who looked like Desperate Housewives without the Botox treatments and Prada accessories.

I realized they were the Wiccans. Not one flinched. But why would they? Whatever spells they cast vanquished the dragon's fire instantly.

Synd circled lazily above me. Why should he worry about *when* to fry me? It was obvious he had more power than I did, and probably far better aim.

My fire song grew more and more faint.

"Liberty!" called Dad.

I didn't have the energy to turn around. I felt so drained. What was going on? I fell to my knees and, though it took a lot of effort, I managed to look up.

I could see my orange-red energy flowing toward Synd's dragon form. His song rose in a crescendo, so loud it made my ears ring. I felt clammy, lightheaded. I was tethered to the blue dragon. He was somehow sucking the life right out of me.

"Dad," I said, my voice quivering. "Do you have a lighter?"

I didn't know why the red dragon was bothering with the Wiccans, when I was obviously the prime target. Maybe it needed toys to play with while Synd killed me. Because I felt very much like I was dying.

Mom and Dad low-crawled toward me. When they reached me, Mom draped her arms around my shoulders. "How can we help?"

You gotta love my parents. They were the ultimate in going with the flow.

My throat clogged. I felt my blood thickening. All the warmth in my body was being siphoned away. "Need. Fire."

Dad flicked a lighter near my fingertips. His hand shook as his gaze met mine. It was obvious he couldn't set his little girl on fire. He looked scared, and that scared me. Dad was never afraid.

"Light. Me."

"Are you sure, honey?"

"Elmore, give me that!" My mother yanked the lighter out of his hand and stuck it under my arm. The tiny flame offered a pianississimo note, so soft I could barely hear it. But it was there. I listened hard and welcomed its song.

"C'mon, Sybina," I whispered. "Don't let your brother win. Don't let us die."

My arm ignited. My mother dragged my father backward, away from me. The fire song surged through me as the flames rejoined my dragon soul. The rope of magic between me and Synd lengthened, getting thinner and thinner. His obnoxious music—Sheesh, what was that crap? Mötley Crüe on an elevator with ten seconds to live?—started to fade.

Synd bellowed and dove toward me.

Chapter 20

Pop! Pop! Pop!
    The blue dragon screeched as it jerked in rhythm to each sharp crack. Several more shots were fired from invisible sources, and each one found a thigh, a wing, a leg. Wailing pathetically, Synd soared up into the inky dark and disappeared.

The red dragon stopped lobbing fireballs at the Wiccans. Roaring, it twisted around and flapped leathery wings double-time to catch up with its retreating companion.

"And don't come back," I shouted, shaking my fist. But I knew they would return, which in an odd way was a good thing because we still needed to get dragon spit.

In front of me, four large green bubbles, all emitting an electric hum, emerged out of thin air. Brady and his three-man rescue team appeared; all were dressed in a strange black material that couldn't be burned, torn, or cut. They also held submachine guns of a make and model that did not technically exist. Both the outfits and the weapons were just more secrets Brady had brought with him from his mysterious government job.

The team surrounded me, Mom, and Dad, and took aim at the sky. If Synd made the mistake of returning, he'd get another round of bullets—hopefully in his big, stupid skull.

Brady stepped toward me and took off his headgear. His face was painted black. His brown eyes looked me over. His form of concern was to ascertain if there were injuries, and if so, how to treat them. That was about it. Brady was not an emotive man.

"You okay?" he asked.

"Peachy," I said. My fire went out, my song shut up, and exhaustion poured through me.

"You're naked," he said. "And your hair's on fire."

I touched the top of my head and felt the heat of the flames still flickering there. I patted them out. Damn it. My body suffered no ill effects from the fire, but obviously I needed to rethink my wardrobe. Where could a girl buy clothes that were dragon-proof?

Without my dragonfire, I got cold, and quick.

Brady removed his flak jacket and slung it over my shoulders. It was heavy but not warm. Then Dad wrapped his coat around me. I was buried to my ankles in snow. Very cold, icy snow.

I shivered and my teeth chattered.

"What's the plan?" asked Brady.

"We get our daughter the hell out of here," said Dad gruffly.

"I think we should stay," said Mom.

"What for?" asked Dad.

"To meet vampires and werewolves. To study this fascinating town. To find out how our daughter became a dragon." She looked at me, her brown eyes twinkling. "What else could you be? But mostly, Elmore, I think we should stay because the nice people headed this way probably won't let us leave."

"Men, move out." Brady dropped his headgear and lifted his gun. "We'll find you and get you out."

He pushed a button on a wrist gadget. In the blink of an eye and a flash of sizzling green, he and his team disappeared.

"Wait!" yelled Patsy. She was followed by Gabriel, Lorcan, and several others. Behind them was a mud-splattered white Mercedes. On the other side of the yard, the triplets were herding the Wiccans into a large paneled truck.

"Oh for fuck's sake!" She marched up to us. "Who were those guys? Where did they go?"

"Brady and his team go wherever they like," said my mother. She was not the kind of woman who could be bossed around by anyone.

"Not in Broken Heart," snapped Patsy. "Call them back now."

Mom turned her dark eyes on the vampire queen. "No."

Patsy's mouth dropped open. It took a full minute for her to grasp my mother's unorthodox response to facing the ruler of vampires and werewolves. Then Patsy's eyes went red and she pointed at Mom.

Mom raised her palm in a "stop" gesture. "Don't bother with the glamour. I'm immune. We all are."

"How the hell—"

"Can we save the interrogation until we get Liberty out of the snow and into some clothes?"

Patsy blinked, her ire cooled by my mother's practicality. "Yeah. Sure."

"Where's the compound?" I asked.

"On the other side of town. Don't worry, Ralph and his boys made it. They're safe." Patsy gestured to Lorcan. "Can you do that wooky-woo stuff and clothe the woman?"

"What the hell is wooky-woo?" I asked, alarmed. I stepped back, my gaze zeroing in on Lorcan. "Does it hurt?"

"No," said Lorcan. "I can create clothing with my magic. Would you like to go somewhere private?"

Well, yeah. I think I'd been more naked in Broken Heart than I ever had at the nudist colony. Quite frankly, the only person in this town I wanted to see me naked was on the other side of town. I was so relieved that Ralph and the boys were okay, and yet a selfish part of me wished Ralph was here. Or I was there. I just wanted to see him with my own eyes.

Lorcan escorted me inside the smoldering house. The kitchen was intact, so we went in there.

"I'm sorry," he said. "I'll have to look at you in order to . . . er, do the wooky-woo."

"Hey, I'm not the one who has to explain it to your wife," I said, shucking off the coat and flak jacket.

He flinched. "Don't remind me."

Lorcan pointed his pale fingers at me, and gold sparkles shot out and wove around me. The first items that appeared were a white lace bra and matching panties. Thick socks and leather ankle boots materialized next, then faded jeans and a brown cashmere sweater. He'd even managed a long wool coat with a hood, and gloves—both a luxurious cream color.

"Wow," I said. "That's the most awesome power I've seen yet. You're like a walking Saks Fifth Avenue."

"You don't know the half of it." He gestured for me to walk ahead of him. I didn't know if he was being a gentleman or just cautious.

When I got back outside, my parents were gone, and so was everyone else. Only Gabriel and Patsy waited near the Mercedes.

"Where's Mom and Dad?" I asked. Trepidation echoed in my voice.

"Don't get your knickers in a knot," said Patsy. "We sent them off to the compound. You can ride with us and tell me what the hell's going on."

Lorcan still walked behind me. Gabriel was on the other side of the Mercedes, his hand on the opened driver's door. Patsy was in front of me, just a couple of feet away from the car.

I don't know why I didn't hear the fire song in time; the fireball that exploded the Mercedes was certainly screeching loudly enough.

Patsy was knocked to the ground in front me. Gabriel flew backward, across the street and into a copse of trees. I had no idea what had happened to Lorcan. Given the blaze, he might be ash. But Patsy wasn't.

I grabbed her by the arms and dragged her away from the burning car. Heat buzzed in my spine and flared out to every nerve ending. Sybina was angry.

So was I.

My whole body quaked with a new power, a different energy I didn't understand and wasn't exactly controlling. I stared up at the creature as the electric heat whipped around me and Patsy.

When I looked up, I saw that the red dragon had

returned. I hoped Synd was bleeding somewhere. And that he was in pain. Not very nice thoughts. Bad karma thoughts, but deserved, damn it.

The dragon flew backward and landed on the street. An Asian woman dressed in red leather slid off its back. Again with the leather! Ugh. She sashayed toward me, her smirk ruining an otherwise pretty face. Her aura was blue. I was beginning to understand the auras seen by my dragon half. Vampires were blue, werewolves were red, and, well, I wasn't quite sure what purple or gold meant yet.

"Who are you?" she asked, though her tone indicated she couldn't care less. Her gaze flicked to Patsy and her smarmy grin widened.

Energy crackled inside me. I felt encased in a tornado of heat, but the swirling power didn't seem to impress the woman. She put her palms about a foot apart. A ball of fire formed in the space between her hands.

"Lia! Don't!"

The shout came from above. A man dropped from the sky, landing deftly between the woman and the bubble of electricity around me and Patsy. I remembered seeing him at the meeting. He was dressed in a T-shirt, jeans, and Converses; his dark hair was savaged by my whirlwind.

"Hello, Ruadan." Lia tossed the fireball at him.

The ground shook under our feet and split open.

From the gap rose a huge wave of water, which doused the fire and soaked Lia. She spluttered angrily, backing toward her dragon. The creature raised its head; smoke curled from its nostrils.

A well-dressed man, shorter than Ruadan, with curly hair and dark eyes, walked toward us. His hands were aimed at the water, and I realized he was manipulating it. I recognized him from the meeting, too.

"Velthur, you ass!" Lia screeched. "Do you know how much this outfit cost?"

I gaped at her. The woman was psychotic. She obviously didn't value life, especially if she wore some poor cow's tanned and colored skin. I bet she had killed the animal she was wearing. Argh! When it dried, I hoped it tightened to the point of cutting off her circulation. Well, if she had circulation.

Following the man named Velthur were three black wolves. The triplets, I was sure. I heard growls and snarls to the left of me; a really huge white wolf loped across the street. Its aura was purple, and I knew it was Gabriel.

The other three lycanthropes surrounded Lia.

"Libby," yelled an Irish voice behind me. Lorcan. He was okay! I couldn't believe how relieved I felt. "You have to stop," he continued to yell, "so we can get to Patsy."

"I . . . I can't," I said. "I don't know how to turn it off."

Chapter 21

The energy bubble grew bigger and bigger. I wasn't in control of it, but I think Sybina might've been. At least I hoped so. All the while, I couldn't take my gaze from Lia. She didn't seem at all concerned that she was trapped by vampires and werewolves.

The white wolf crouched in front of me, howling. He couldn't get near us. I realized Gabriel was crazy with worry.

"She's unconscious, but alive," I called. "We'll be okay."

He barked, his paws digging at the ground by the edge of the electrified field.

Lia was dripping wet, but she hadn't lost her smirk. Her dragon lifted its head and shot fire at Velthur; he aimed the water at it and smacked it in the head. The dragon choked and sputtered, then lay on the street, as if defeated.

Ruadan stalked Lia, who retreated even closer to her dragon. Velthur kept his hands pointed at the gushing water, obviously ready to use it when needed.

Ruadan made two short swords appear in his hands. They were gold and bejeweled and very, very sharp. He swung them expertly, dancing closer to Lia.

Lia responded by creating two swords of her own, but hers were made of fire. The flames highlighted the wild look of her dark eyes.

"Is that any way to treat your wife?" she asked sweetly.

"Ex-wife," said Ruadan. "Don't do this, Lia. What do you hope to accomplish?"

"You never were ambitious, Ruadan. You, who are the child of gods, would rather live in harmony with humans. You should rule them!" She punctuated her words by slashing at him with her fire blades.

He dodged easily.

I heard Synd's evil, screaming song. Shit. He came at us with full fire; blue-green sparks of his magic ribboned within the flames. The blaze shot toward Velthur and turned the water into steam. The vampire wasn't deterred, even though it was obvious to me that throwing water bombs at the new threat was taking its physical toll. I stared at Synd; something wasn't quite right with him. His fire song sounded weird and I couldn't see his aura.

"Get out of here, Velthur," shouted Lorcan. He flew over us. Oh, yeah. He was part Sidhe—fairy. He, too, held a sword, this one made of gold light. I guess he could magic more than clothes.

I looked down to check on the queen. She was still passed out. I squatted and brushed her hair away from her face. As *loup de sang*, I knew she would have a heartbeat and breath. I checked her carotid pulse and sighed with relief. It was strong. If she'd wake up, she might be able to kick Lia's ass so we could all go home. And I really wanted to get away from all this freaking craziness. Once again, I found myself thinking about Ralph and the boys. Maybe a normal life was too much to hope for a vampire, a half-dragon, and two adorable toddlers, but I think we could get really damned close.

If I survived. I was tired of dragon attacks. I wanted them to be gone. For good. I wanted to know Ralph, Michael, and Stephen would be safe. They wouldn't be—not so long as these dragons lived.

Velthur's gaze flashed to us. I sensed his exhaustion more than I saw it. He wasn't going to last much longer. As Lorcan went for Synd's scaly hide with his blade, Velthur turned and took off so fast he was a blur. I didn't blame him. He couldn't help us, even if he continued to risk his own life. The water splashed to the pavement, leaving only a muddy hole.

Synd circled lazily, as if he had all the time in the world to turn us into crunchy bits. I was terrified of him in a primal way, like a child who fears imaginary monsters lurking in the dark. Only my monster was real and my inner child was screaming her head off.

Lorcan couldn't get near the beast, even though he kept trying to stab it. The dragon soared up, shooting green fire at him.

Lorcan was forced to retreat.

Synd floated higher and higher. The farther away he got, the better I felt. Synd's presence was evil. I had never really believed in evil before. People could be mean, they could make bad decisions, and yeah, even harm others. But that dragon—he felt dark and empty. He had no conscience. We lived at his pleasure.

Why had he flown away? And how the hell had he healed so quickly? Or had he? Something was off about him, like he was an astral projection.

Lorcan landed on the ground, outside the fighting zone of Ruadan and Lia. He kept an eye on the dragon, his sword at the ready.

The three wolves circled Lia and Ruadan as they parried. Neither one was really getting in any blows.

I was rooting for Ruadan in a big way. Sybina seemed to agree. I felt her clamor. She built our combined rage into more power. The force field expanded and encompassed the white wolf and, beyond him, Lorcan.

Gabriel went to his wife and nuzzled her face, whining. The bubble of protection intercepted Ruadan and one black wolf.

"Damnú air!" cried Ruadan, running toward the electric field. He bounced off it. "Let me out!"

"I can't," I said. "Sorry!"

Lia's face lit up in triumph. She extinguished her swords and backed away from the encroaching bubble. The wolves on either side of her advanced; they growled and bared their teeth.

She extended her arms. Two fireballs shot out from her palms and struck the wolves.

They fell to the ground, yelping in pain. The fire ravaged their sleek black fur as they rolled and rolled, trying to get the flames out.

Laughing as if she'd just performed a delightful magic trick, Lia whirled and ran to the red dragon, climbing its side.

"You'll soon know what real power is," yelled Lia. "Don't worry, Ruadan. You'll still have a place in the new order. As my slave!"

The red dragon rose into the air and flew upward. Lia was *not* getting away. The power inside me felt like a lightning storm trapped under my skin. I closed my eyes and tapped into my years of visualization experience. I imagined a ball of light forming between my hands. I saw the light, felt its heat, held its weight. Sybina helped me. For the first time since she'd given me her power, I felt like a dragon.

When I opened my eyes and looked down, the ball was there, as big as a basketball and as bright as the sun. The fire was mine to create, to control. My magic was within it, and my intention to protect myself and the innocents.

The dragon roared. I knew at any moment it would dive on us and try to burn us all to a crisp or rip us apart with teeth and claws.

I made the light bigger and brighter.

"What are you doing?" Ruadan hurried toward me, his expression one of horror. The swords fell out of his hands and clattered to the muddy ground. He collapsed to his knees and rolled away, shielding his face. His skin started to peel away, wisps of smoke fluttering into the air.

Oh, my God.

"Sybina," I whispered, "you have to stop. Please. We *have* to stop."

The fire was singing. It was happy. It had purpose. I couldn't divert it or extinguish the ball of light.

"Dad!" cried Lorcan as he shot toward the fallen man. The light pulsing in front of me immediately took its toll on Lorcan. He ducked, putting up an arm to protect his face. His hand erupted in tiny flames. "It's too bright. You're going to kill us!"

There was only one way to get rid of the dangerous weapon I'd created.

I lobbed it at the red dragon.

The orb struck the dragon's underbelly and exploded. The creature screeched as the assailing light consumed it; Lia's screams mingled with her pet's ear-splitting cries.

The creature fell at least thirty feet, smacking into Ralph's house with a force that knocked me off my feet. I heard the crackling explosion of wood and the chinkle of shattering windows.

The dragon crawled out of the rubble and collapsed halfway into the mangled front yard.

I sat up, staring at the large body as its blackened skin smoldered. In some places, it peeled off. It was mewling, obviously in terrible pain. Regret stabbed me. What had I done? I wouldn't eat or wear the skin of any creature, and here I had tried to kill one.

Then I thought about those two sweet little boys and I wasn't as sorry. I'd do anything for them and their daddy.

"What have you done?" asked Ruadan, echoing my own thoughts. My gaze went to him and Lorcan. They had already healed, which surprised me. I had figured they would need an infusion of blood.

Ruadan climbed to his feet and helped his son to stand.

"I stopped her," I said, though my voice held no conviction. I also got to my feet and dusted snow off my coat. Now that all the fires had been put out, my hands were cold. It seemed like winter had infiltrated my clothes and slithered under my skin.

"You attacked an Ancient," said Ruadan. He sounded both angry and shocked.

"I don't understand," I said. "What's an Ancient?"

I really should've read all of my mother's books. I vaguely recalled her telling me vampires were separated into different sects, which all had different powers. But I was fuzzy on the details.

"She saved us, Dad," said Lorcan. He turned to me. "For more than four thousand years, the first seven vampires have existed. We don't know what would happen if the founder of a Family died."

Ruadan nodded. "You may have killed more than just Lia. You may have destroyed every vampire in her Family."

Chapter 22

"What do you mean?" I gulped. I don't think any penance would be enough if I wiped out a bunch of vampires because I couldn't control my inner dragon.

Ruadan and Lorcan studied me, their faces mirrors of worry. Well, I was worried, too. I'd let Sybina have too much control. I knew I'd have to come to terms with this new side of myself or figure out a way to get rid of it.

Behind Ruadan, I saw a very naked Damian checking on the two werewolves. They sat together, licking their singed fur, their eyes glazed with pain. Ruadan and Lorcan turned toward them.

"My brothers are okay, but they need care," said Damian. "I will take them to Brigid."

I wasn't sure how he planned to transport his injured brothers. It looked like they were going to have to limp out of here. Then I realized that Ralph's car was untouched in the driveway.

"Take the Honda," I said. "I don't think Ralph would mind."

"Um, Libby?" said Lorcan gently. "About Ralph—"

"No, seriously. He'd want to help. And if he gets mad, I'll take the heat for it." I rushed to the car, relieved that it was unlocked. I didn't have the keys, but once again I put my skills to work and in seconds the engine turned over.

Damian hurried toward me. I tried really hard to keep my eyes above the waistline. The man was built like a linebacker and all the parts were spectacular. It was stupid to even be thinking about it, but naked men could be very distracting.

"Thank you, *Liebling*." He leaned close and whispered, "You saved us all. Every battle has a sacrifice. I'm not at all sorry that Hu Mua Lan is dead."

"Thank you," I said. I was immensely grateful for his words. I didn't exactly feel better about frying two living (or whatever) beings. However, it seemed werewolves weren't nearly as melodramatic as vampires.

Damian nodded to me, and then drove the Honda to his brothers. He loaded them gently into the car and left.

Ruadan and Lorcan had walked behind me,

ostensibly to check on the queen. I didn't want to look; I didn't want to see more condemnation. Or another naked man. I had heard the shifting sounds and knew Gabriel was probably in his human form.

"How's Patsy?" asked Ruadan.

"She's still unconscious," said Gabriel. Yeah, he was naked. "Lorcan, can you take her back to the house?"

"Of course."

I heard the terrible *snap-snick* sound and ventured a look over my shoulder. The white wolf stood next to Lorcan, who scooped Patsy into his arms. Lorcan and Patsy shimmered away until nothing was left but a few magical sparkles.

The wolf stared at me with its golden eyes, and I felt bad all over again. They'd lock me up and throw away the key. My parents, too. I wouldn't see anyone again—ever.

To my shock, Gabriel bowed to me, lowering his head until his snout almost touched the ground. Then he turned and loped off.

"You have his thanks," said Ruadan. "Maybe even his respect."

Well, that was good news. Better than the suspicion that I had blown up a vampire who'd been around for four millennia.

I was quaking inside and out, from anxiety and the release of the energy. Mom told me that every

224

choice exacted a price. It was the way the universe kept balance.

"Come with me. We must assess the damage." Ruadan gestured at me to follow him and we headed toward the dragon.

The smell of burning flesh was horrific. Bile rose as the fumes attacked us. The star-bright ball I'd created had just about cooked the dragon. It was still alive, but very weak. Its gaze followed us, but it didn't try to attack.

"Lia?" called Ruadan. He sounded almost tender.

I stopped, staying well out of reach of the dragon's claws. The beast had landed on its side. I couldn't see Lia. If she'd survived the blast, she might've fallen off. My heart turned over in my chest. What if I had killed her?

Well, that had been my intention, right? My stomach clenched as guilt settled in it like a lump of lead.

Ruadan lifted into the air and drifted over the dragon. He landed on the other side. After a minute or so he floated up a few feet and looked at me, his expression inscrutable. "She's not here."

I wasn't exactly relieved to know Lia had escaped the fireball. She was still dangerous, especially when paired with Synd. I hadn't wanted to be responsible for her death, but I didn't exactly want her capable of wreaking more havoc, either.

"Can she do the *Star Trek* thing, too?" I asked.

Ruadan nodded thoughtfully. "Yes. All the Ancients have that ability. It's possible she beamed herself to safety and left the dragon to its fate."

Nice to know Lia was consistently evil. The dragon hacked pitifully, and I felt sorry for it.

"Well," said Lorcan next to me, "we should probably get the dragon spit."

I screamed and turned, whapping him on the shoulder. My heart pounded furiously. "Shit! Could you please stop doing that?"

"Sorry," said Lorcan, his lips curling into an almost smile. "Me 'n' Dad can pry open its jaws. You collect the saliva."

I stared at him. "With what? Because I'm not sticking my hand in there and just . . . scooping."

"Anything left in the kitchen?" asked Ruadan.

Dutifully, I climbed through the debris and picked my way through the demolished kitchen. Nearly every dish and glass was broken. After digging through a few piles, I managed to find a plastic measuring cup.

Lorcan looked at my find with a raised eyebrow. "That's for dry ingredients."

"Thank you, Martha Stewart." I seriously wanted to whap him again. "I hope a half cup of dragon spittle is enough."

Ruadan got on one side of the dragon's massive head and Lorcan on the other. It didn't protest at all as the vampires grabbed its jaw and pried it open.

It belched and the smell of sulfur and death rolled over me. I gagged. Blech.

"Any day now," said Ruadan.

I kneeled down and leaned toward the mouth full of big, sharp teeth. Slowly, I reached inside. It flicked its slimy tongue over my arm.

"Ew! Ew!" I jerked away. "Gross!"

"Did you get any?" asked Lorcan.

"No," I said. I shouldn't be so squeamish. After all, Patrick and his wife were sick because of me. I owed them this much. Once again, I stuck my hand inside and pushed the cup under the big, floppy tongue. Oh. Yuck. I scooped and dragged it back out. Dragon spit was yellow and noxious. Carefully, I stepped back until I was completely clear of the beast.

"Is there anything we can do for it?" I asked.

"You can release it from its mortal form," said a voice behind us.

I turned around and saw Ash standing nearby watching us.

"Ash," said Ruadan, irritated. "Where have you been?"

"Trying to find Synd's hidey-hole." Her gaze traveled over the massive beast, who was wheezing hard now. Black blood dribbled out of its nostrils and mouth.

Ash looked at my soaked arm and my precious

cup filled with one-third of the restorative for dragon poison.

"Here," I said. "You can use it for the cure."

"Why would I use demon spit?" she asked. She looked at the three of us and laughed. "That thing's not a dragon. It's a demon. Lia must've bound him into the form of a dragon. Jeez. He's really milking the death scene." She glanced at me. "Demons are immortal. They can't be killed, only sent back to hell."

I stared at the dragon that was not a dragon. Demons were real, too? I shouldn't be surprised. I should just assume that every creature in every myth was real. Then I wouldn't get a shock every time one showed up.

Now that the demon had been found out, it stopped with the labored breathing and rolled onto its belly. It stretched out, then put its head down, closing its eyes. Oh my God. It was taking a nap. I guess it didn't have feelings.

Ruadan took a cell phone from his front pocket and dialed a number. "Damn it. Battery must be dead. Lorcan?"

Lorcan offered his cell phone, but after Ruadan dialed, he shook his head. "It's not working, either."

Ash flipped open her phone and frowned. "Mine's dead, too."

What fresh hell was this?

I was so tired, I didn't care. And I was still holding demon spit. "Do we need this?"

Ash shook her head. "Demon anything is bad juju." She opened her pink jacket and unzipped a pocket. To my amazement, she pulled out a Ziploc bag filled with brown stuff. I saw spots of red in it, and at the top, the glitter of gold. "I found leftover vampire by the melted swing set in the backyard."

Ruadan took the bag and unzipped it, sticking his hand inside. I realized I was still holding the demon saliva, so I dropped the cup onto the ground. "How did you get that big-ass bag into your coat?"

"Let's just say I know a fashion wizard with some mad skills."

Ruadan lifted a delicate gold necklace from the bag. The pendant was a magnolia blossom. "I gave this to Lia for our first binding. My mother made it from fairy gold. It can't be destroyed."

For a moment I couldn't speak. I examined the ashes and saw the strips of red leather. "She's . . . dead?"

"Yes." His voice was hard. He didn't look at me as he clenched the necklace in his fist.

Apologizing was so inadequate. How was I supposed to phrase it? Sorry I killed your murdering, conscienceless ex-wife? Well, it was worth a shot.

"Ruadan, I'm sorry."

"I know." Ruadan looked at me, and I was

surprised to see empathy lurking in his silver gaze. "I know you did what you did to help us all. You couldn't have known what might happen if Lia died."

"Oo-kay." Did this mean he was forgiving me for killing his ex-wife?

Lorcan took my hand and squeezed it between his own. "Darlin', Ralph is part of Lia's Family."

I processed what he was trying to say. His earlier words floated through my scrambled thoughts: *You may have killed more than just Lia. You may have destroyed every vampire in her Family.*

Oh, my God.

I had murdered Ralph.

Chapter 23

"You have to take me to him," I yelled. "Right now!"

Lorcan looked taken aback. "Maybe you should calm—"

I grabbed him by the shirt, yanked him close, and glared at him. "Take me to Ralph *now*."

"Libby, if something's happened to Ralph, perhaps it would be best—"

Men with their moron logic and patronizing tones. Or maybe it was the vampire in Lorcan making him stupid. I spun around and started off in the direction of the compound. Lorcan grabbed my shoulder.

"If Ralph . . . if he died, those boys are alone! They need me. Now either do your sparkly bullshit or let me go."

"Okay, Libby," he said.

"Don't worry about us," said Ash sarcastically. "We'll just stay here with the stank-assed demon."

Like I cared. I was anxious to get to the compound.

"We'll have to get Phoebe," said Ruadan. "Other than Patsy, she's the only one with demon powers."

The dragon snored. It was either the laziest demon around or so tired of Lia's ownership that hell was a welcome retreat.

"C'mon," I said impatiently. My stomach roiled, and I pressed a shaking hand against my belly. I wouldn't feel okay until I knew the truth about Ralph's fate.

Lorcan embraced me. One moment we were standing in the front yard of Ralph's destroyed home, and the next——*twinkle, twinkle, don't throw up*—we arrived outside a white building.

I still felt like my molecules were being reassembled, but I didn't want to take an extra second to steady myself. I yanked open the door and barreled through it.

Lorcan followed me into the lobby. I had no idea where the hell we were. I turned around, slammed into the vampire, and wobbled backward. "Where are we?"

"The Consortium's headquarters. C'mon." He took the lead and I hurried behind him. We entered a wide hallway and headed toward a set of dark wood doors at the end.

My heart hammered. Had Ralph turned into ash? Were the boys even now weeping for their father? I couldn't bear the thought.

Lorcan opened the doors and we entered a huge, brightly decorated room. The primary colors, comfy sitting areas, bookshelves, and myriad of games pegged it for a rec room. I saw my parents in the corner, sitting on opposite sides of a table with a chess board on its middle.

They both got up, their gazes showing relief.

I didn't recognize most of the people milling around. I saw Patsy, Gabriel, Damian, and Velthur. Yeah, all but the three faces I wanted to see most.

"Ibby!"

I whirled around and there were Michael and Stephen barreling toward me. And behind them, their father. Their handsome, kind, sexy, very much undead father. Relief rushed through me, and the tears I'd managed to keep at bay flowed freely.

I squatted down and the boys ran into my open arms. I hugged them and kissed their little blond heads. Ralph kneeled down and cupped my face. His fingers caught my tears, and his gaze was filled with much more than relief. I saw love there. I cried harder.

He kissed me, not in a gentle missed-you kind of way, but in a reaffirming, passionate never-leave-again way that stole my breath. My heart.

"You squishing me, Daddy," groused Stephen.

We broke apart, grinning stupidly at each other.

"Oh, God, Libby," he said. "I thought you were . . . " His gaze fell onto the boys, who looked up at us with wide eyes.

"Yeah," I said. "Me, too." I wiped my eyes with a sleeve. "I look terrible."

My coat was ripped, my ass was sore from being thrown across the snow-filled yard, and my eyes felt puffy from crying.

"You look beautiful to me," said Ralph.

Oh, he was sooooo getting some. I licked my lips, and his eyes dropped to my mouth. I wanted to be alone with him, to show him just how much he meant to me.

"Honey?"

My dad's voice put the kibosh on any more thoughts about hot monkey love. Ralph and I stood up and faced my parents. The boys clung to their father's legs, and their father put his arm around me. I scooted closer and slung my arm around his waist. I could see that the others in the room had congregated near a large sitting area. Lorcan had found his wife and was talking to the gathering. I figured he was telling them about Lia—and what I'd done.

"The phones are out here?" I asked.

"Yes," said Ralph. "None of the cell phones work. The land lines in Broken Heart were disassembled months ago."

Mom and Dad shared a significant look. Great.

Brady was probably the reason the phones didn't work. That man had been busy. Was he still intent on rescuing us? I bet that my parents had a way to contact him, but were waiting to see how things played out. Either that, or Brady wasn't the one responsible for cutting off the cell phone signals.

"I'm Ralph Genessa. These are my sons, Michael and Stephen."

Ralph stuck out his hand, which my mother took. "Theodora Monroe, and this is my husband, Elmore." She looked down at the boys. "Hello."

"Hi," said Michael.

Stephen blinked at her and stuck his fist into his mouth. Gawd, they were cute.

Dad shook hands with Ralph, too, and I could see that my father was sizing him up. Elmore Monroe was the strong, silent type, with emphasis on the silent part. Ralph must've met his approval. "Nice to meet you, son."

"You, too, sir."

"You mean you guys didn't talk the whole time?" I asked.

"I just got here," said Ralph. "The compound has temporary housing, and we were assigned one of the bungalows. The boys were hungry and needed a bath." He looked at me. "And I needed to keep myself busy. When you didn't come back right away—"

I nodded, feeling myself tear up again.

"Daddy, play blocks," said Michael.

Stephen nodded.

"Okay," said Ralph. "But don't throw them at your brother."

Giggling, the toddlers took off to a pile of big plastic cubes.

"The vampire queen is fascinating," said Mom. "And she has the most extraordinary vocabulary."

"She means that Patsy has a keen ability to use a certain word as an adjective, verb, noun, and once even managed an adverb," said Dad. "A commendable feat."

"C'mon," said Mom. "You look exhausted."

She led us to a cozy sitting area near where the twins were playing. Mom and Dad each took a chair. I took off my coat, draping it across the table in front of me, and then sat down. Ralph sat partially on the armrest and put his arm over my shoulder while I leaned against him.

I knew my parents were probably wondering what was going on with me and Ralph. It's not something I wanted to explain, especially since I didn't really understand it myself. Love seemed such a simple thing in books and movies. Two people were meant to be together. Every obstacle was climbed, torn down, or blown up—and, ta-da, happily-ever-after.

But love was so much more than just moon-eyed looks and tearing off each other's clothes. Love was terrifying. It was falling off a cliff. It was stepping into shark-filled waters. It was sacrificing to a pagan goddess who demanded blood.

And I had done all those things. Gladly.

I told my parents everything that had happened since I set foot in Broken Heart. With a few Ralph-sized omissions. Ahem. Well, I only told them everything up until the part where I fried Lia, and her demon dragon crushed the rest of Ralph's house.

"Aren't you surprised about Archie? Well, Stanley," I asked my mother. I couldn't quite work up the nerve to talk about Lia yet. Though from the looks we were getting from those on the other side of the room, I knew Lorcan had told them an earful. Shit.

"Oh, you can't hold his nature against him," Mom said softly. "He's a curious man with a wonderful intellect. I'm sure he meant you no harm when he took you for testing."

My mother believed everyone was good-hearted. It was one of the reasons Theodora Monroe didn't feel the slings and arrows of cynics and snobs. She regularly befriended people who didn't always have the best intentions. And if they stole from her or conned her or insulted her, she treated them just the same as if they'd been kind to her. I had never mastered this way of dealing with people.

"What about the fact that he faked his death?"

"Well," she said, her eyebrows drawing down. "I suppose we should've appreciated him more."

"Oh, Mom. Jeez." I rolled my eyes. But really, Stanley was the least of my problems now. I fiddled with the sleeve of my sweater. "Okay, look. I sorta accidentally killed Lia, who's one of the seven Ancient vampires. And the dragon is really a demon, but I didn't find that out until I scooped out its drool."

Mom, Dad, and Ralph all stared at me. Then Ralph said, "You killed Lia?"

"She was trying to kill everyone else." I sounded defensive. I inhaled a steadying breath. "I somehow made this ball of sunlight, and then I threw it at the dragon. Well, the demon. Lia turned to ash. Ruadan said destroying an Ancient might destroy her whole line."

"We know it's not true," he said. "I'm from her Family and I'm still here."

"I believe in the sacredness of life, Ralph. I'm a vegan because I hate the idea of something dying so that I can live. And yet, I created that . . . that weapon and threw it at two living creatures."

"To save your life and the lives of others."

"I still don't feel good about it."

"Nor should you. But it's done now, Libby. All you can do is move forward."

"He's right, Liberty," said my mother gently.

"Your guilt will not help the one who passed from this world. You were brave and strong."

"We're proud of you," said Dad.

I felt as though boulders had been lifted from my shoulders. The people I loved forgave me. They understood. And even though I wasn't too keen on what I had done, I could live with it. Especially because it meant those sweet little boys would be safe.

At least from Lia.

Synd . . . not so much. He was a bigger problem. One that needed to be solved or we'd all pay the price—with our lives.

Chapter 24

"Libby?" I looked up and saw Lorcan standing nearby. "The queen would like to talk to you." His arm was around a teenaged girl who was dressed in black. She had black-rimmed eyes and an eyebrow ring. Her hair was as shiny and dark as a raven's wing, except for two cherry-red stripes on either side of her face. "This is Tamara. She'll watch the boys."

"She will?" I asked.

Her eyebrows went up, giving emphasis to the silver ring.

"She's a great babysitter," said Ralph.

"Yeah," said Tamara. "I do all my Satanic rituals after the kids are asleep."

"*What?*"

Lorcan laughed. "She's teasing, Libby."

"Thanks for watching the boys, Tamara," said Ralph in a choked voice.

Suspicious, I looked at Ralph. Yep. He was laughing, too. He got up and helped me to my feet. I looked over my shoulder and saw Tamara sit down next to the boys. She caught my gaze and waved. It didn't make me feel any better. I felt very protective of Stephen and Michael.

We all traipsed over to the other side of the room. Mom and Dad squeezed in next to Lorcan and Eva on a yellow couch. Ralph and I took a blue, puffy chair. Once again, I sat down and he leaned on the armrest.

Ruadan and Ash had joined us and there, hiding behind Damian, was Stan. He was such a chicken-shit. I saw Zerina, too, and a few others I didn't recognize. This was quite the get-together.

Everyone quieted and looked at Patsy, who sat on the center couch with her husband, Gabriel. She opened her mouth.

"I'm so pleased to meet all of you," burst out Mom. She turned solicitously to the queen. "How are you feeling, dear?"

"Fine," said Patsy. She looked flummoxed. Well, Mom did that to people a lot.

"I'm so glad to hear it. And just think, if my daughter hadn't saved your life, you wouldn't be sitting here now." Mom tsk-tsked. "Not to mention what might've happened to your poor babies!"

Did Mom know how to give a warning tucked into warm fuzzies or what? I bit my lip to keep from grinning. Mom was probably the only human around who wouldn't be instantly cowed by vampires and werewolves. And dragons.

"Libby kicked ass," said Patsy. She glanced at my mother. "Would you like me to high-five her?"

"Maybe later," said Mom.

Gabriel snorted a laugh, which earned him a pinch on the leg from his wife.

"It's getting close to dawn, so let's just get down to brass tacks. Libby killed Lia. I ain't too sorry about it. I've wanted to blow that bitch up since the day I met her." She waved off the various reactions, which ranged from gasps to chuckles. "Lorcan and Eva used their übergeek powers to ferret some info. I'm the new chief of the bloodsuckers and the wolfies. So, even if killing an Ancient once meant the end of a Family, it doesn't anymore."

"And if someone kills you?" asked Dad.

"We'll just make sure that doesn't happen." Patsy rubbed her belly. "So, wanna tell me why you all can't be glamoured?"

"Why do you need to know?" asked my mother.

Patsy gave her an are-you-serious look, and Mom responded with a damn-right-I-am look.

"Fine. Do us all a favor and ask your invisible A-Team to come out and play nice."

"Nope. They're our insurance," said Dad pleasantly. "You keep us safe, and you stay safe."

His pronouncement had the same effect as if he'd said, "We think you eat babies."

"Wait just a damned minute. We don't go around killing decent folks," said Patsy. Her voice vibrated with indignation.

"Um, hello? Didn't you tell me I couldn't leave Broken Heart?" I asked. "And then you threw me in vampire jail."

Patsy had the grace to look uncomfortable. "You blew up my living room. And you can't control your dragonfire."

"Now, now," said Mom. "We don't need to rehash the past. Queen Patricia, we do understand the nature of your citizens. We know that you need secrecy to survive. We have no intention of telling anyone else about Broken Heart."

"You'll forgive us if we seem skeptical," said Gabriel.

"I've gone toe-to-toe with Michael Shermer," Mom responded. "I can handle the skepticism of a *loup de sang*."

"Here's the thing," said Patsy. "I don't like the idea of your guys running around my town. Nobody's safe as long as Synd is still alive. So call them in, and we'll figure out a plan together."

Mom and Dad looked at each other, then at me. Mom shook her head. "Like you said, it's getting close to dawn. Let's all get some rest, and discuss it in the morning. Er, evening."

"It would be better to strike at Synd now," said Ash. "He's vulnerable. With a day's rest, he'll be at full strength." She pointed at me. "She's not a vamp."

"No, she's your bait," said Ralph, his arm going around me protectively. "She's exhausted, and I'll be damned if I let her out of my sight again."

The independent woman in me protested his high-handed territorial behavior. But the girly-girl in me told the independent me to shut the hell up. I snuggled closer to Ralph.

Everyone looked at us. Patsy's gaze stayed on us the longest. Finally she said, "Is there something we should know?"

"Yes," said Ralph. He cupped the back of my neck and said, "I claim you, Liberty Monroe."

I felt heat spiderweb up my neck. I looked up at Ralph. What had he just done? Well, other than tell everyone here that we were a couple.

"Liberty," said Mom. "Have you mated with him?"

"I . . . uh . . . that is . . . " I swallowed the knot in my throat, blushing furiously. "Yeah. Well, sorta."

"You two did the nasty?" demanded Ash.

Ralph and I stared at her. I couldn't answer, but Ralph did.

"That's none of your business."

"You did." She put her hands on her hips and laughed. "Oh, Jesus. Do you have tattoos? A circle with two slanted lines?"

"How did you know that?" asked Ralph.

"Because I'm the leading authority on dragons in this room. You've bonded."

"You did the vampire hitch?" asked Patsy. Her eyes goggled at Ralph. "Holy shit."

"There was no hitching," I said. My gaze flew to Ash as my heart started to pound. "W-what does that mark mean?"

"Two souls become one," explained Ash. "Although since you both have some of Sybina's soul, it's more like two half souls reuniting." She shook her head. "I've never come across this situation, but whatever. You two are married."

"Married?" I squeaked. My heart tripled its beat as a lead weight settled in my stomach. I couldn't look at Ralph. I didn't want to see his expression. What if he was in for the nookie, but not up for a very long-term relationship? I was, though. I didn't care how insane, irrational, or illogical it sounded. I wanted to be with Ralph and the boys. And forever suited me just fine.

"How do you unbond?" asked Patsy. "Or is there a time limit? Vampires are only bound for a hundred years."

Ash snorted. "Dragons don't *unbond*. They mate for life."

A wave of horror washed over me. "I bonded." I swallowed hard. "With Ralph. But I'm a human."

"Your dragon half is stronger," said Ash. "You've got strength, fire magic, and you're damned near immortal. You can't fly or shift, but hell, that part's no fun anyway."

"But we didn't . . . I mean not—you know, all the way."

"Doesn't matter," said Ash. "It's the heart of a dragon that chooses his mate. FYI, you can't poison Ralph."

"Poison?" I asked faintly. I was still shell-shocked. And what about poor Ralph? I got up the courage and slanted a glance at him. He looked as discombobulated as I felt.

"You're both half-dragons. So if Ralph drinks from you, you won't poison him."

I hadn't thought about Ralph sinking his fangs into me. I wasn't sure how I felt about being his lover and his meal.

"How did this happen?" The question came from my father, and his tone was not friendly. Neither was the look in his eyes.

"I'd rather not go into details, sir," said Ralph. He looked at Ash. "When you say for life . . . "

"Sorry, dude. Dragon mating trumps vampire bonding. There's none of that wiggy shit where your mate suffers the same fate as you do. Libby is your wife until one of you dies, which for you two is a really, really long time." She threw her hands up in the air. "Look, I don't care if you two boink each other stupid. I have another problem. If I don't get Synd tonight and take his soul, I can't stick around."

"A soul shifter?" Mom studied Ash. "I didn't think you existed."

Coming from Mom, that was saying something.

"I'm hurt. Really." Ash blew out a breath. "I have to take a soul every ninety days, and it's not like I have a choice. I can't control my nature. When it's time to absorb a soul, my physical form takes over. There's no controlling it or reasoning with it or stopping it. *Capiche?*"

"Yeah," said Patsy. She looked queasy. I wondered if it was because of her pregnancy or because of Ash's soul-sucking. "Just don't forget to get his spit before you whack him. It's the only way to help Patrick and Jessica." She rubbed her eyes, sighing. "Let's just get some rest, and do another one of these fun, fun meetings tomorrow. And Dora, if there's any way to contact your . . . *insurance*, then tell 'em to stand down, okay?"

"Agreed," said Mom.

The meeting broke up. Ralph helped me from the chair.

As we headed toward the boys with my parents in tow, Lorcan and Eva joined us.

"Dora and Elmore, we have accommodations for you," said Lorcan.

I glared at him. "Oh, really? The kind with glass and bossy electronic voices and too much of the color white?"

"Whoa, now." Lorcan put his hands up in a surrender gesture. "They're in the bungalow next to Ralph's."

Eva smiled. I liked her. She was nice and seemed less intense than most of the vampires I'd met, with the exception of Ralph. "How about we take Stephen and Michael for a slumber party?"

Ralph took my hand and squeezed. "Thanks, Eva."

"How in the world are the vampires supposed to handle two mortal children?" asked Mom. "What if they wake up? Or have a tummy ache? Or need a glass of water?"

"Tamara is—" started Eva.

"No, no," said Mom, waving away objections. "We'll be happy to watch the boys."

"I'd be thrilled if you and Elmore would watch the boys," said Ralph.

"Excellent! Now, go away and let us play with our grandsons."

Grandsons. I couldn't believe how easily Mom and Dad accepted Ralph and me as dragon-mates. Married by almost-sex. My stomach clenched. Oh. My. God.

There wasn't a get-out-of-mating card. Ash said a dragon's heart chose its mate. Had Ralph and I chosen each other?

Or had Sybina chosen for us?

Chapter 25

Eva and Tamara said good night. Lorcan walked them to the door, but when they went through it he stayed with Damian. I figured they'd been assigned to escort us to the bungalows. Queen Patsy wasn't taking any chances.

While my parents sat down and played blocks with the twins, I drew Ralph aside.

"You claimed me, in front of my parents and the Broken Heart mafia."

Ralph smiled. "I'm not usually so He-Man, I promise. We're bound, Libby." Panic flashed in his blue eyes.

"It's too late to get cold feet," I said. I took his hands. "I don't care what Ash says. Nothing is ever written in stone. If you want to find a way out of this—"

"No." He kissed me. "I'm all in, Libby."

I'd told him that yesterday, and I meant it, too. It was scary-crazy, but I had no intention of changing my mind.

Ralph looked down at me and I saw love shining in his eyes. How was it possible to fall in love that fast? We'd skipped all the regular courting rituals and dove right into forever marriage. Screw it. I didn't know much about those rituals and I'd never been the type of girl to follow society's mores. Who said I couldn't fall in love with a vampire, marry him, and raise two beautiful boys with him?

I looked down at my parents. Dad held Stephen as they stacked blocks into a tower. Mom helped Michael push over the house they'd just built together. It was like they were already a family.

"We know what we know," said Mom. How was it that the woman always knew what to say? "I met your father in Reno, Nevada, at a UFO convention. I married him the next day."

"What?" I stared at her, openmouthed. "You never told me that."

"I listen to my heart, Liberty. It has never steered me wrong."

And that was why Mom's faith in the paranormal, in the goodwill of people, and in love was so damned unshakable. It didn't matter if my dragon half or my human half had chosen Ralph as my mate. My heart was still mine and it said: Ralph's the One. Go for it.

Mom made shooing motions. "Go on. We'll take the boys to our bungalow when we're done playing."

I leaned down and kissed Mom on the cheek. Then I kneeled and gave Dad a hug. He pulled back, tears in his eyes. "We love you, Liberty. And we're happy for you."

"Thanks, Dad."

I felt teary yet again, so I stood up and let Ralph lead me away.

"You have the greatest parents," he said. "I mean, *wow*."

"Yeah," I said, grinning. "Wow."

Lorcan walked us to the bungalow. I had no plans to leave Ralph's side, much less Broken Heart, but I guess the man had his orders.

"Congratulations," he said. "And good luck."

We said good-bye. I was getting nervous now. We were going to bond-*bond*. All the way. My belly squeezed as anticipation wriggled through me.

The bungalow reminded me of Ralph's destroyed home. It was cozy, or would've been had it not been drenched in white and missing the personal touches that made a house a home.

Ralph kissed me, and everything in my world felt absolutely perfect.

"Why the smile?" Ralph asked. "Something make you happy?"

"Yeah," I said. "You do."

Ralph took me into the bathroom and undressed me slowly. I returned the favor. He did nothing more than hold me under the warm water. We washed ourselves from hair to pinkie toes.

As the water went cold, our bodies went hot. It was probably wise to stay in the shower, considering we wouldn't light the tiles on fire. At least, I didn't think we would.

"I've already claimed you," he said. "Now we just have to do the word-giving, and the . . . you know." He waggled his brows.

"What's the word-giving?"

"Something like . . . 'I love you, Libby. I promise to honor, respect, and protect you to the best of my ability.'"

"You forgot to say that you'll obey me," I said, feeling all gooshy.

He grinned. "I think we'll both skip that one." He brushed my hair away from my face. "Your turn."

"I love you, Ralph. I don't know what the future holds for us and our rather diverse family, but I look forward to the journey." I put his palm over my tattoo. "My heart beats for you."

"And mine would beat for you," he said softly. "If it could still beat."

I laughed, and then he dragged me close and

kissed me. Whoa. He sucked my tongue into his mouth, flicking, swirling. I groaned and he swallowed the sound.

I rubbed against his pectorals. My nipples hardened as his chest hair abraded the sensitive peaks.

My hands were everywhere on him, touching, stroking. My ability to think faded and I felt immersed in his smell, his taste, his touch. I dragged my lips across his throat, tasting his collarbone before swiping the muscled contours of his chest.

Desire pulsed in every part of my body. Ralph slipped one finger inside and smiled. "You are so wet."

"Duh. You are so hot."

He rewarded my compliment by rubbing my clit. He nipped my earlobe. "I love you."

"I love you, too."

He cupped my buttocks and lifted me. I wrapped my legs around his waist and held onto his shoulders. *Oh, yes.* He pushed his cock against my wet heat.

I panted and moaned. Ralph slid his cock between my slick folds, making sure he bumped my clit with every stroke.

He bent his head and sucked one of my nipples into his mouth. He laved the tight bud, scraping his teeth across the tip.

Ralph paid lascivious attention to my other nipple.

"Please," I begged. "Please!"

He rubbed his cock harder and faster until my pleasure built higher and higher. And then ... boom! I imploded. Or at least it felt like I had.

Ralph positioned his cock at my entrance, pushing just inside it.

Breathing hard, my limbs quivering, I looked at him. He put his mouth against my neck. My skin tingled where his lips brushed.

At the same time his fangs pierced my flesh, he drove his cock inside me. My maidenhead tore. I don't care what they say in romance novels: It fucking hurts.

Ralph drank my blood, gripping my buttocks as he made slow thrusts inside me. The penetration felt strange, but soon pleasure built again.

Ralph stopped drinking and pressed his forehead against my shoulder. He thrust harder and deeper and all I could do was hang on.

Another orgasm claimed me. Then Ralph groaned and came, his thighs trembling as his seed filled me.

I was officially married to Ralph.

I was a stepmother, too. I hadn't thought about motherhood before, but I liked the idea. A lot. Me ... a mom.

Dragon, vampire, human ... it didn't matter. I felt our bonding all the way to my soul.

*   *   *

I woke before Ralph did. I snapped on the lamp and turned to look at him. His chest didn't rise or fall. His skin looked waxy. Still, he was a very cute dead man. He'd tugged on pajama bottoms last night, but had forgone the shirt at my request.

I felt naughty feeling him up while he was still resting, but that nudge of guilt didn't stop me from running my palm along his muscled contours. I traced the tattoo. That was weird. A third line had appeared in between the two slanted ones. It was as long and thin as the other two, but a vibrant red. I looked down at mine and saw that I had the same red line. What did that mean? Maybe only that we had done the mattress mambo as dragon mates.

I kissed his cheek, then got out of bed. I took a shower and got dressed. Maybe I'd ask Lorcan to magic up some new duds. I went to the kitchen and made myself some coffee. As it perked, I looked out the window. It was already dusk, but I could still see the fresh snow on the ground.

I checked on Ralph, who remained dead to the world. I chuckled. I didn't think I'd ever get tired of making vampire puns.

I sat on the couch and turned on the television. It was a rerun of *The Princess Bride*. Oh, I loved this movie.

A few minutes later, I heard the bedroom door open and Ralph shuffled into the living room. He looked at me, grinning. My heart skipped a beat.

Ralph snuggled with me on the couch and we finished watching the movie. Ralph kissed my neck, which made me forget about everything except what I wanted him to kiss next.

I took off my sweater and Ralph unsnapped my bra. His eyes were drawn to my tattoo. He traced the red line. "What does it mean?"

"I don't know. Maybe it's a gold star for being so good in bed."

He rewarded me for that comment. Things got *really* good. So good my heart started knocking hard against my chest. Thump. Thump. Thump.

Ralph looked up from nuzzling my breasts; his eyes were glazed. I imagine his delirious expression matched my own.

"Do you hear that, Libby?"

"Yes," I breathed, drawing him down again. "It's my heart. It's trying to beat out of my chest."

Thump. Thump. Thump.

He looked up again and frowned. "No. I think it's the door."

We both sat up. I groaned in frustration.

"You better put on your clothes."

I resnapped my bra and put on the sweater. Ralph used his fingers to comb through his hair, then went to answer the door.

"Libby," called Ralph. "It's your parents."

I went to the front door and peeked over Ralph's shoulder. Mom, Dad, and the twins crowded onto the front porch. My libido cried, "Unfair!" But I was still happy to see my family.

While Ralph took a quick shower and got dressed, I settled with my parents and the twins in the living room. Mom and Dad hugged me and then I hugged the twins. My parents had brought bags of toys with them, and the boys sat on the living room floor and played contentedly.

"Can I get you anything?" asked Ralph from the doorway. His hair was still damp and he was, unfortunately, fully clothed. I thought about what was under those clothes, and my pulse stuttered. Ralph's blue eyes found mine and he raised one eyebrow. Ah. He heard my heart race and had figured out what I was thinking.

Ralph's cell phone rang. Surprised, he took it out of his pocket and looked at the display.

"We contacted Brady," said Mom. "He stopped jamming the cell phone tower. He agrees that he shouldn't come in until we've spoken to Queen Patsy."

"And that's who's calling," said Ralph. My gaze followed him as he walked out of the living room. Hm-mmm. Look at that ass. I caught myself ogling and straightened.

Ralph reappeared in the entry way.

"We're meeting in the rec room. Tamara's coming to watch the boys."

"Okay," I said, suddenly anxious. "What's going on?"

Ralph tucked the phone back into his pocket. His worried gaze connected to mine. "Ash found Synd's lair."

Chapter 26

When we arrived, Tamara was waiting for us near the rec room door. I hugged the boys and gave them sloppy kisses, and Ralph did the same. She took Michael and Stephen to the play area.

People were still milling around, obviously waiting for the meeting to begin. My parents joined the fray, talking to anyone who would talk to them. I noticed that Stan tried to stay out of their way. He wasn't going to escape my mother, no matter how hard he tried.

I saw Ash leaning against a wall, looking impatient and bored. She wore an outfit that reminded me of the Bride's from the *Kill Bill* movies. It was one piece, fit her like a second skin, and was obnoxiously pink. Her boots were pink, too. I never figured an ass kicker like her would choose such a girly color.

Since the queen hadn't arrived yet, I dragged Ralph over to Ash.

"Our tattoos changed," I said. "After we . . . uh, consummated our relationship."

Her eyebrows rose. "Changed how?"

"There's a red line now, in between the two slashes." I elbowed Ralph in the side. "Show her."

He rolled his eyes, but lifted his T-shirt. I noticed that her eyes skated along his abs before settling on the tattoo. I didn't have time to gouge out her eyeballs, though. Her eyes widened and she smirked at us.

"Shit. I don't believe it." She patted our shoulders. "Congratulations. It's a girl."

"What?" Ralph and I shouted at the same time. We looked at each other, stunned.

"You mean she's pregnant?" He put his hand on my belly, like he could figure out if there was a baby growing there. "Really?" His voice had gone soft.

"Uh, no," I said. "I was a virgin. And he's dead."

"He's also a dragon." She held up her hands. "Don't ask me how the hell he managed to get his swimmers to work. I'm not a biologist. Dragons are lucky if they get any kids out of a mating. It's one of the reasons they're so rare these days." She nodded toward my still-flat stomach. "The one growing inside you will probably be the first dragon born in . . . oh, about five hundred years."

"Libby's pregnant?" asked Patsy. She had just entered the room and was less than a foot away from us. "How is that possible?"

"Not a biologist," said Ash.

"Shit." Patsy grimaced. "I mean, congrats." She looked at Gabriel, who stood next to her, and then she looked at Ash. "This changes everything. We can't ask her to draw out Synd now."

"What?" snapped Ralph. "I already told you she wasn't going to be used as bait!"

"C'mon, Ralph! We weren't going to douse her in barbecue sauce and throw her in his cave."

Ralph turned his gaze to Gabriel. "Would you let your pregnant wife do something like this?"

"Not in a million years."

Patsy turned and glared at her husband.

"That is, I'm not the boss of her and I always support her choices."

She smiled and faced us again. I saw Gabriel look at Ralph and shake his head slightly. Patsy thought she had the upper hand in that relationship. But it was obvious that Gabriel would go to extreme measures to protect her—whether she liked it or not. And by gauging Ralph's reaction, he probably felt the same way.

I was with Patsy. I should have a choice. And my choice was . . . not to do it. I didn't want to be dragon bait. I heard the boys giggle and looked over my shoulder. But I would do it for them. Synd would keep striking at us, at everyone in Broken Heart, until he got what he wanted.

Even though Ash was the only one who could stop him, I was probably the only one who could get her close enough to draw him in.

"I don't see why we can't use her," said Ash. "He won't go for Ralph because he doesn't know that Ralph has part of his sister's soul."

The debate raged, but I drifted away mentally. There was a baby growing inside me. A little girl. Would she have scales? Or look human? Was there a *Raising Dragons for Dummies* book out there? We'd have to fireproof the nursery. And her brothers. Yowzer. Ralph had given me one hell of a wedding present. I pressed a hand against my belly and grinned like an idiot.

"Right, Libby?"

Ralph's strident question pierced through my pink cloud of thoughts. I blinked at him, taken aback by his fierce gaze. "What?"

"You're not going. I don't care how much backup they have. I won't risk you." His gaze dropped to my stomach and I saw equal measures of worry and wonderment. He hadn't had time to absorb the idea. "I won't risk our baby, either." He gulped, then glared at Ash. "You're sure about this?"

"Christ! I'm *not* a biologist or a fucking doctor. I just know what the dragon symbols mean."

"Hey, boss, I got the shields ready." We had been joined by a short brunette who had sparkling green eyes and a dimpled smile. She wore denim overalls, hiking boots, and a thick coat. Her hair was braided into pigtails, which stuck out from under a ball cap she wore backward. She smelled like gasoline. Oil smudged one pristine cheek.

"Hey! I'm Simone Sweet." She pumped my hand enthusiastically. "Nice to meet ya."

"Nice to meet you, too."

She nodded toward Patsy and headed back out the door. "What shields?" asked Ralph.

"Simone runs the garage, but she's also a whiz with metallurgy. She made some metal shields for the more flammable people to hide behind," said Patsy.

I knew someone who could trump metal shields.

"We could bring in Brady," I said. "If I used one of the force fields, it would give me extra protection."

"Libby." Ralph gathered me into his arms. "Please, tell me that you're not considering this crazy plan."

"We won't be safe from Synd. Not ever. Not the boys, not you, and not me or our baby." I broke away and looked at Ash. "Can you get him?"

"Yeah," she said. If I didn't know better, I'd think

it was respect that glimmered in her diamond eyes. "You're damned right I can get that bastard."

February sucked.

The wind blew hard, slicing at my face like razors. I put my head down and kept going. The air was bitter cold. Without streetlights or moon to offer light, the darkness seemed as thick and black as tar.

Four of us crept along in the woods. Ash was the assassin in charge. Lorcan had the happy task of cultivating dragon saliva. Ralph refused to stay behind. He held my hand like I planned to float away any second.

Ash had turned down the opportunity to use the surprisingly light metal shields created by Simone. But Lorcan and Ralph each had one.

Brady had agreed to come in, but refused to bring in his team. Before we left on what he called a suicide mission, he clipped a small black device on my coat. All I had to do was push the button and the shield would appear. It would not only make me invisible, but offer protection against fire, claws, and teeth.

Ash led the way, since she'd figured out which cave the dragon used. Lorcan was behind her. Then me and Ralph.

Maybe we should've been looking up.

Hands gripped my shoulders and, before I could

take a breath to scream, I was being yanked up into the air. I saw Ralph's horrified expression, and then Synd wrapped an arm around my waist and took off like a shot. I realized he was in human form except for his big, iridescent wings.

I couldn't reach the button to enact the shield. I fought like a madwoman. I wasn't going to die, damn it. I kept kicking at his legs and tried to bite his scaly arms.

I bashed the back of my head against his face. He screamed in agony and dropped me. I managed to push the shield button.

An electric hum filled my ears and a bubble appeared around me. I bounced along the ground and rolled to a stop. My heart stuttered and sweat dotted my brow. I was so scared, but I fought the urge to throw up.

Synd floated to the ground and stalked around, obviously looking for me.

No one else was in sight. How far had we gone from the dragon's lair? Several yards away I saw the grave of Therese Genessa. Talk about coming full circle. This was where it had all begun. And where it would all end.

I needed Synd to be able to find me so Ash could find him. With shaking fingers, I punched the button again.

He stepped toward me and raised one hand. I watched in horror as his fingers morphed into deadly, sharp claws. "I have no desire to bargain with stubborn females."

"Too bad, asshole," said Ash as she just . . . popped out of thin air. I stumbled backward as Synd whirled to face his nemesis.

Ash advanced on him. She held a wicked-looking sword with practiced ease. My thought was that an Uzi would get the job done faster.

"Burning down my hotel didn't kill me, stupid," she said, swinging the sword with an incredible grace. "But you did manage to torch my favorite shirt, and that pisses me off."

I had no intention of watching the two of them battle. Ash scared me nearly as much as Synd did.

I scrambled to my feet, ready to hightail it the hell out of there. Before I could take a step, Synd waved his hand at me, and I found myself a living statue. I couldn't move, though it didn't stop me from trying. Sweat dripped off my temples, but no amount of mentally demanding that my muscles move got them to do the job.

Synd and Ash didn't talk much, just tried to kill each other. The dragon turned both hands into claws and used them as effectively as ten tiny daggers. Every time he made contact with Ash's clothing, his claws bounced off. He didn't leave a mark.

The same could not be said for Ash's neck and left cheek. She never cried out, never got angry. She was a machine of efficiency. Synd had an ego the size of Canada. He had bulk and he had the ability to shift into a very dangerous creature.

But Ash was the better fighter.

Synd couldn't accept defeat. He went after Ash again and again, getting more and more desperate. At one point Ash took a tiny blade from . . . well, somewhere, but I had no idea where she could possibly store anything in that outfit.

She tossed it at Synd's neck. The blade seemed to be alive; it burrowed into his skin. The dragon slapped at the spot where it had entered, screaming.

All of Synd's dragon manifestations reverted. "No!" He clawed at his neck as if doing so could make whatever the object was come out again.

"Don't worry," said Ash. "You're still a dragon. You just can't go all scales and fire on me."

Completely naked, his skin gleaming with sweat, Synd sank to his knees.

"You haven't won," he said savagely. "I've lived more than two thousand years!"

"That's long enough, don't you think?"

Ash swung her blade toward his neck.

Chapter 27

"Ash!" Lorcan appeared in a shower of gold sparkles and he was clutching Ralph. "*Damnú air!*"

"Fuck." Ash kept her blade against Synd's throat. He snarled and tried to stand. She kicked him in the balls. He wailed and fell to his side, clutching his genitals.

My husband ran toward me and grabbed my shoulders. Relief shuddered through me.

"What's wrong, honey?"

I couldn't tell him. I couldn't speak or move. I couldn't even feel the beat of my own heart.

"Don't worry," he soothed. "I'm right here. It's okay."

"The change is coming," Ash said through gritted

teeth. "Get what you need and then get the hell out of here."

Lorcan kneeled down and pried open Synd's jaw. I heard a popping sound that made my stomach lurch. I didn't see what Lorcan took. I was grateful that his sample was tucked into an opaque container.

"Is she okay?" he asked.

Ralph nodded. "Go. Get the cure for Patrick and Jess. We'll be all right."

Lorcan disappeared and Ralph stood in front of me, putting his arms around me awkwardly. He pressed his shoulder against my face.

I couldn't see. But I could hear just fine.

The sound of Ash's blade sliding through Synd's flesh reminded me of the butcher's knife hacking off a hunk of beef. If I wasn't already a vegan, I'd commit to the lifestyle immediately. The whole thing sickened me.

The magic binding me dissipated and I fell to the ground, my limbs shaking. I kept my eyes shut tight, but I felt the light beating against my eyelids and felt a wave of heat roll over me.

I pushed out of Ralph's embrace and, despite the warning bells clanging in my mind, looked.

The headless body of Synd lay on the ground. Ash stood before it, at least a dozen long blue lights circling her body like electric eels.

Hollowly, she looked at us. "No. Soul."

She sounded as if the words had been torn out of her mouth. She walked toward us jerkily, like her body was moving her along without permission. "Need. Soul."

Realization was sudden and terrifying. Synd didn't have a soul. Ash had initiated the process of absorption. She couldn't stop it.

She needed a soul.

Oh, God. I hated the idea of losing my life, and the life of my child. It was so goddamned unfair. But those two little boys were alive and well and had already lost their mother. I couldn't let their father sacrifice him for me.

I pulled the force field device off my jacket and stuck it onto Ralph's shirt. Then I pushed the button.

He went invisible. I shoved him away, as hard I as could. I forgot I had dragon strength. A few yards away I saw a neatly trimmed hedgerow part. Safe. Ralph was safe.

Ash reached me in mere seconds. She grabbed my hands, and held on to me. The blue lights crawled onto me. I started to burn from the inside. I felt pulled and twisted. My feet went numb first, then the numbness climbed into my calves and inched up my thighs.

My vision started to gray. I was dying.

"Libby!"

Ralph's voice. Damn it. Couldn't the man take a

hint? My vision swam, but I recognized his blurry face.

"What are you doing?" Ralph yelled at Ash. "You're killing her! Stop!"

No one could touch me, especially not Ralph. I knew he wanted to, and I wished he could. I really wanted him to hold my hand. I wanted to feel loved . . . one last time.

Then, suddenly, I was free.

Without Ash trying to suck the soul out of me, I could breathe again. My whole body burned and ached. I'd never been in so much pain before.

"Ralph?"

He was gone. I staggered to my feet and turned around.

Ash was standing face-to-face with Ralph. Her hands gripped his shoulders as the blue worms of light wiggled onto him.

I saw the moment his soul popped free. The orange-red ball of pure energy floated into the center of Ash's chest.

Then the lights solidified and Ralph's body was encased in the pulsing blue. Ash's eyes were empty, and I knew that she had no control over what was happening.

A mist formed around Ralph that was sucked into Ash's opened mouth.

Then it was all over.

Ash woke up from her trance. She stumbled

away, weaving like a woman who'd drunk too much tequila, and then she bent over and vomited.

Tears crowded my throat and seeped from my eyes. Ralph lay on the ground. I hurried toward him and fell to my knees. I collapsed on top of his chest and sobbed.

He'd given more than his life for me. He'd given his very soul.

"Ralph," I cried. "Oh, Ralph."

"What . . . happened?"

I jolted upward and stared down at him. His eyes were open and his gaze was on me. "You're alive."

"Undead," he said. He grimaced. "I feel like I've been put through a wood chipper."

"I know the feeling."

"C'mere." He kissed me, then pulled back. "By the way, never, ever do anything like that again."

"I love you, too."

"You're not off the hook," he grumbled. "I still don't get why I'm not dust."

We looked at Ash, who was sitting down with her head between her knees.

"I got your half of Sybina's dragon soul," she said in a raspy voice. "You're all vampire again."

"I thought you killed the people whose souls you take," I said.

"I do. Don't ask me why your man is still able to walk around." She looked up at us, her lips tugged into a half smile. "I'm not a biologist."

* * *

We returned to the rec room. Ralph hadn't let go of my hand, not once. I felt protected and safe. We sat on the blue sofa amid a bunch of paranormal folks who were very glad to see us alive. Stephen sat on my lap sucking on his fist. Michael squirmed on his father's, plucking at his T-shirt.

"You know what would be really great?" said Patsy from her spot on the yellow couch. "If we could live in this town without some kind of asshole trying to off us every couple of months. I'd like to raise my kids without fearing for their lives every day."

"We could build a shield for the town," said Brady. He leaned against the wall, his eyes on all the exits. Ash was doing the same thing, but on the other side of the room. She hadn't said much since we'd gotten back.

"I can manipulate fire, make water dance, send demons back to hell, fly around the sky, bend metal, talk to ghosts, shift into a wolf, and glamour others," said Patsy. "But I still can't make a whole town invisible."

"I could do it," said Brady.

All eyes turned to him.

"Dora says we're staying. So, we're staying."

"Okay," said Patsy. She looked at me, my parents, and Brady. "Welcome to Broken Heart."

Chapter 28

Three months later . . .

"Everything's normal," said Dr. Merrick as she stared at the monitor.

I lay on the examining table, my shirt pushed up to reveal my rounded tummy. Gel was smeared all over it, and Dr. Merrick merrily pushed her little wand all over my abdomen. Ralph stood next to me, holding my hand.

"Scales?" I asked. "Is there smoke in there? Or is she covered in fire?"

"No," she said, chuckling. "Most shifters deliver their babies in human form. I can't say what's going to happen once the baby arrives. I've never dealt with dragons."

I had already been imagining fire-filled burps

and dragon gas that would set off fire alarms. Ralph and I were building a new house where the old one had stood. It wouldn't be finished until the summer, but it would be bigger: five bedrooms and two and half bathrooms. We had also made plans for a swimming pool and a fort for the boys. Everything would be fireproof, including our clothes. Like Dr. Merrick said, no one had dealt with a baby dragon in a long time. Five hundred years, if Ash was right. The idea of raising our dragon daughter was both terrifying and exhilarating.

I never thought of Ash as the sentimental type, but she'd been the first to send along gifts for the baby. Her fashion wizard had created some very cute flame-retardant baby clothes. And even Brady had offered to make us some useful items from his strange techno-whatsits.

Dr. Merrick turned the monitor so it faced me and Ralph. We both peered at the image. I could make out the teeny tiny form of a baby. Oh my God. I squeezed Ralph's hand as excitement did handstands through me.

Dr. Merrick pointed to a little pulsing circle. "The heart," she said softly. "Very strong. Healthy."

We stared at our baby girl. There she was, against all odds (An undead dad and a dragon mom? Can you say therapy?), growing inside me.

"Wow," I said, looking up at Ralph.

"Yeah," he said, grinning. "Wow."

He leaned down and kissed me. His golden aura had turned red. From dragon to vampire, thanks to Ash. He didn't have fire, not since she'd taken his dragon soul. Without the answering passion of his dragon to ignite me, we didn't set anything on fire. All the same, we'd switched to a platform bed custom made by Brady. I wasn't sure what the bed was made out of, but it looked like that carbonite stuff Han Solo had been frozen in. The mattress was out-of-this-world comfortable. More importantly, it couldn't be set on fire even if you poured gasoline on it and threw on a lit match.

Ralph's cell phone rang. My heart skipped a beat. The boys were staying with their favorite babysitter, Tamara. I was still anxious about leaving them. After all, I was their mother. A duty I shared with Therese, whom we visited every Sunday. I would make sure the boys knew their birth mother. That was the thing about love—it had no limits.

"Is it Tam?" I asked anxiously. "Are the twins okay?"

I had found that parenting held a lot of joy, frustration, and fear. I was constantly worried about Michael and Stephen, especially when they weren't with us.

Ralph looked at the phone display and frowned. "Nope," he said. He flipped it open. "Hello, Patsy." He paused and his eyebrows shot upward. "What? Well, okay."

He ended the call and looked at me. "She says we have guests, and to get to her house pronto."

Dr. Merrick gave me some paper towels to wipe off my belly. While I got dressed, Ralph went with her to schedule the next appointment and to get a refill of my prenatal vitamins.

Twenty minutes later, we presented ourselves at Patsy and Gabriel's mansion.

Patrick opened the door.

I gave him a hug and he returned it lightly. Vampires had quite the squeeze, so they had to be careful. Patrick and his family had become our good friends. We'd spent many a Friday night with him and Jessica and their children.

Anyway, I'd turned into a hugger. My hormones were whacked out and I felt either really affectionate or really weepy. Everyone got hugged, even the scary werewolf guys. They were a sucker for a pregnant woman's embrace.

"What's up?" I asked as Patrick led the way into the living room. It had been rebuilt and refurnished. Patsy had thanked me, saying my accidental demolition had been an unexpected help in the decorating process.

"You'll have to see it to believe it," said Patrick. He stopped and let me and Ralph go ahead of him.

Patsy sat on an oversize black velvet couch. At seven months pregnant, she was the picture of health. Or to hear her tell it, the freaking picture of when-will-these-children-get-out-of-my-aching-womb exhausted.

On the opposite couch, which was also oversized and velvet, but rather an eye-popping red, sat a teenaged boy and two older women. The auras of the females were gold.

"Dragons," I whispered.

In the middle was a tall woman dressed in blue robes. Her silver hair was plaited into a single braid that was so long it was piled on the seat behind her. Her eyes were an odd shade of blue-green. I could sense her fire. My eyes were drawn to her gold-rope necklace, and to the fire red jewel that rested just above her bosom. I heard it singing. I didn't recognize the song, but knew it was ancient, primal.

On the left side of this imposing woman was a teenaged boy. He wore black jeans, a Cure T-shirt, and studded black boots. His eyes were black. Not dark brown. Black. So was his hair, which fanned over his scalp in a Mohawk. His eyebrows, lips, and nose were all pierced. His aura told me he was a human. He sure kept odd company. Or maybe it was the dragons keeping odd company.

My gaze shifted to the woman on the other side of Silver Hair. She was older, too. She looked in her early sixties. She wore a crocheted white sweater with a purple dragon on it, pink knit pants, and thick-soled orthopedic shoes. Her lilac eyes were filled with excitement.

"Hello, Libby," said Silver Hair. "I'm Raine. This is Amethyst."

"Oh, my! It's such a pleasure to meet you, m'dear. When we heard about your pregnancy!" She twittered and clapped her hands. "Oh, my!"

I wasn't sure how to respond. "Ash said dragons were rare."

"We are. There are less than a hundred of us left. And no one has mated, much less conceived a child, in the last five hundred years."

"How old are you?" I asked.

Amethyst's eyes widened and she clapped a hand over her mouth. Oops.

"I'm sorry," I said hastily. "I shouldn't have asked."

"I don't mind," said Raine, giving Amethyst a fond smile. "I'm the Eldest. I've walked the Earth for the last three thousand years. Amethyst is a few hundred years younger, give or take."

"Three thousand *years*?" I gulped. "Holy shit."

Raine nodded. "You have much to learn about your new heritage." She rose and took off the necklace. "I am here to offer you and your mate my blessing. Your child has a great destiny."

"That's all we need," said Patsy, her tone sarcastic. "Destiny sure has been busy knocking up a lot of women lately."

Raine's gaze went to her. "Perhaps you should consider why so many were drawn to Broken Heart. Why the fates of three peoples are so closely connected."

Patsy rolled her eyes.

Raine put the necklace on me. "Within you grows the last dragon of the Oriana line. Sybina and her brother were the youngest of our kind, and they have crossed into Yalinia. Heaven."

"Not Synd," I said. "He didn't have a soul. Is there a dragon hell?"

"Yes, though we do not speak its name." Raine frowned. "Ash told us about Synd. It is most troubling." She looked at me, her lips curving into a smile. "No worries. This necklace holds within it ancient dragonfire. Its magical properties will protect you. When the time is right, you will give it to your daughter.

"And we have another gift for you, a talented trainer who will teach you our ways and help when the young one is born."

Dread plunked into my stomach. My gaze turned to the boy who looked like a punk band reject.

"Rand has lived with dragons his whole life. He knows everything, and it is customary for a dragon to have a sijin."

"Right," I said. "I wouldn't want to be without one of those."

Rand got off the couch. His black gaze studied me and then Ralph. He held out a hand and we shook.

"Where do I bunk?" he asked.

"I think we'll need a few new additions to the house," I told Ralph.

Patsy laughed. She took her husband's hand and kissed his knuckles. Her gaze met mine. "Never let it be said that Broken Heart is boring."

With my parents integrating into the community, Brady and Stan building an invisible force field the size of a few football fields, and several hybrid babies on the way, *boring* would be the last word I'd use to describe Broken Heart.

For all its weirdness, there was only one word to describe this crazy town I'd come to love.

Home.

PRIS Founders Honored
at Memorial Service
by Susan Rickerson, *Tulsa Tribune*

Theodora and Elmore Monroe, their daughter, Seraphina, and longtime friend Braddock Hayes, were honored yesterday by friends and family at a memorial ceremony held on a private Florida beach.

The Monroes were founders of Paranormal Research and Investigation Services, or PRIS, and were well-known investigators of the supernatural.

The four PRIS members went missing after their Cessna 350 crashed in the Gulf of Mexico. Despite an exhaustive two-

week search, neither the plane nor sur-
vivors were recovered.

"We are deeply shocked and saddened
by the loss of our friends," said Ingrid
Dellingham, a longtime PRIS member
and now full owner of the organization.
"We will carry on their work."

Dellingham put together several psychic circles and séances, hoping her lost
friends would contact her from the Other
Side.

"I think their work was done," said
Dellingham. "And they had no reason to
stick around, especially since Seraphina
was with them."

Dellingham says she and her team will
go to Oregon, as the Monroes would've
wanted them to, to investigate the area
where Bigfoot sightings have been ram-
pant.

"Well, they're a migratory population,"
said Dellingham. "When they move on to
their new nesting area, there's always a
rash of sightings."

THE SEVEN ANCIENTS

(In order of creation)

Ruadan: (Ireland) He flies and uses fairy magic.

Koschei: (Russia) He is the master of glamour and mind control. He was banned to the world between worlds.

Hu Mua Lan: (China) She is a great warrior who creates and controls fire. She was killed during her attack on Queen Patricia.

Durga: (India) She calls forth, controls, and expels demons. She was banned to the world between worlds.

Velthur: (Italy) He controls all forms of liquid.

Amahté: (Egypt) He talks to spirits, raises the dead, creates zombies, and reinserts souls into dead bodies.

Zela: (Nubia) She manipulates all metallic substances.

GLOSSARY 1

A ghrá mo chroi: (Irish Gaelic) love of my heart

A stóirín: (Irish Gaelic) my little darling

A Thaisce: (Irish Gaelic) my dear/darling/treasure

Cac capaill: (Irish Gaelic) horse shit

Damnú air: (Irish Gaelic) damn it

Deamhan fola: (Irish Gaelic) blood devil

Draba: (Romany) spell/charm

Draíocht: (Irish Gaelic) magic

Droch fola: (Irish Gaelic) bad or evil blood

Gadjikane: (Romany) non-Gypsy

Filí: (Old Irish) poet-druid

Filíocht: (Old Irish) poetry, i.e., verbal magic

Ja: (German) yes

Liebling: (German) darling

Glossary 1

Loup de Sang: (French) blood wolf

Mo chroi: (Irish Gaelic) my heart

Muló: (Romany) living dead

O zalzaro khal peski piri: (Romany) Acid corrodes its own container.

Roma: (Romany) member of nomadic people originating in Northern India or Gypsies considered as a group

Romany/Romani: (Romany) language of the Roma

Solas: (Irish Gaelic) light

Sonuachar: (Irish Gaelic) soulmate

Strigoi mort: (Romany) vampire

Tír na Marbh: (Irish Gaelic) land of the dead

GLOSSARY 2

Ancient: Refers to one of the original seven vampires. The very first vampire was Ruadan, who is the biological father of Patrick and Lorcan. Several centuries ago, Ruadan and his sons took on the last name of "O'Halloran," which means "stranger from overseas."

Banning: (see: World Between Worlds) Any vampire can be sent into limbo, but the spell must be cast by an Ancient or, in a few cases, their offspring. A vampire cannot be released from banning until they feel true remorse for their evil acts. This happens rarely, which means banning is not done lightly.

The Binding: When vampires have consummation sex (with any living person or creature), they're bound together for a hundred years. This was the Ancients' solution to keep vamps from sexual intercourse while blood-taking. No one's ever broken a binding.*

---

*Johnny D'Angelo and Nefertiti's mating was dissolved by a fairy wish. It is the only known instance of a binding being broken.

The Consortium: More than five hundred years ago, Patrick and Lorcan O'Halloran created the Consortium to figure out ways that parakind could make the world a better place for all beings. Many sudden leaps in human medicine and technology are because of the Consortium's work.

The Convocation: Five neutral, immortal beings given the responsibility of keeping the balance between Light and Dark.

Donors: Mortals who serve as sustenance for vampires. The Consortium screens and hires humans to be food sources. Donors are paid well and given living quarters. Not all vampires follow the guidelines created by the Consortium for feeding. A mortal may have been a donor without ever realizing it.

Drone: Mortals who do the bidding of their vampire Masters. The Consortium's Code of Ethics forbids the use of drones, but plenty of vampires still use them.

Family: Every vampire can be traced to one of the seven Ancients. The Ancients are divided into the Seven Sacred Sects also known as the Families.

Gone to Ground: When vampires secure places where they can lie undisturbed for centuries, they "go to ground." Usually they let someone know where they are located, but the resting locations of many vampires are unknown.

Loup de Sang: Commonly refers to Gabriel Marchand, the only known vampire-werewolf born into the world. He is also known as "the outcast." (see: Vedere Prophecy.)

Lycanthropes: Also called lycans. They can shift from a human into a wolf at will. Lycans have been around a long time and originate in Germany. Their numbers are small because they don't have many females, and most children born have a fifty percent chance of living to the age of one.

Master: Most Master vampires are hundreds of years old and have had many successful Turnings. Masters show Turn-bloods how to survive as a vampire. A Turn-blood has the protection of the Family (see: Family or Seven Sacred Sects) to which their Master belongs.

PRIS: Paranormal Research and Investigation Services. Cofounded by Stanworth Industries heiress Theodora and her husband, Elmore Monroe. Its primary mission is to document supernatural phenomena and conduct cryptozoological studies.

Roma: The Roma are cousins to full-blooded lycanthropes. They can only change on the night of the full moon. Just as full-blooded lycanthropes are raised to protect vampires, the Roma are raised to hunt vampires.

Seven Sacred Sects: The vampire tree has seven branches. Each branch is called a Family, and each Family is directly traced to one of the seven Ancients. A vampire's powers are related to his Family.

Soul shifter: A supernatural being with the ability to absorb the souls of any mortal or immortal. The shifter has the ability to assume any of the forms she's absorbed. Only one is known to exist, the woman known as Ash, who works as a "balance keeper" for the Convocation.

Taint: The Black Plague for vampires, which makes vampires insane as their bodies deteriorate. Consortium scientists have had limited success finding a true cure.

Turn-blood: A human who's been recently Turned into a vampire. If you're less than a century old, you're a Turn-blood.

Turning: Vampires perpetuate the species by Turning humans. Unfortunately, only one in about ten humans actually makes the transition.

The Vedere Prophecy: Astria Vedere predicted that in the twenty-first century a vampire queen would rule both vampires and lycans, and would also end the ruling power of the Seven Ancients.

The prophecy reads: *A vampire queen shall come forth from the place of broken hearts. The seven powers of the Ancients will be hers to command. She shall bind with the outcast, and with this union, she will save the dual-natured. With her consort, she will rule vampires and lycanthropes as one.*

World Between Worlds: The place is between this plane and the next, where there is a void. Some people can slip back and forth through this "veil."

Wraiths: Rogue vampires who banded together to dominate both vampires and humans. Since the defeat of the Ancient Koschei, they are believed to be defunct.

NOTE FROM THE AUTHOR

I don't drink milk anymore. I don't care what the American Dairy Association tells you, milk does *not* do a body good: www.notmilk.com.

Unlike Libby, I am not a vegan or a vegetarian. I like meat, from steak to salmon. I pay more for organic, free-range, grain-fed, hormone-free, antibiotic-free, and/or wild-caught meat because I abhor the idea of factory farming. Animals are treated cruelly, and the meat taken from these poor creatures is dangerous to the health of humans: www .themeatrix.com.

Do I even need to mention how important it is to eat organic produce, and to be wary of how much processed food you eat? If you can, go to farmers' markets and support stores that offer locally grown produce: www.localharvest.org.

The Institute of Transpersonal Psychology is a real college: www.itp.edu. So is the HCH Institute: www.hypnotherapytraining.com.

If you don't know who Dr. Michael Shermer is . . . uh, do you live under a rock with the Mongolian death worm? Or in a loch with Nessie? Hah. He's the founding publisher of *Skeptic* magazine: www.skeptic.com.

Finally, the book Libby chooses from Ralph's collection is a real novel. Jeff Strand is also a real person. No, really. I've met him and everything. *Graverobbers Wanted (No Experience Necessary)* is one of my all-time favorite reads. Andrew Mayhem rules: www.jeffstrand.com.

Read on for a sneak preview of
the next adventure in Broken Heart

OVER MY DEAD BODY

Available May 2009 wherever books are sold
and on penguin.com

Saturday, June 14th

"That's a very fine ass," whispered Her Royal Highness Patricia Marchand. "A definite ten."

More like an eleven. My gaze had been roving the object of our mutual assessment for the last five minutes, which was how Queen Patsy caught me. But after taking a gander at the jeans-clad buttocks of Braddock Hayes, she seemed to understand why my gaze was Superglued to the view.

"Simone Sweet," said Patsy under her breath, "you have a naughty streak."

I only smiled. I might be dead, but my eyes—not to mention various other parts—still worked. Granted, certain parts hadn't been in use longer than others, but that was okay by me. Vampires had to be finicky about that sort of stuff anyway. Having sex meant saying "I do" for a hundred years.

No, thank you.

Patsy and I returned to watching the scenery. She was married to a very hot man named Gabriel and in fact probably shouldn't have been ogling Brady. Not that I was gonna to tell her to stop.

Even though it had been dark for at least an hour, it was still ten degrees hotter than hell. Winter had stretched on and on, clawing greedily into April. Spring had lasted all of ten seconds. The heat had rolled in, sucking all the joy out of the smallest breeze. Now, it was the second week of June, and we'd been afflicted by the roasting heat that usually tormented us in August. Since I was a vampire, I wasn't sweating buckets. I didn't have to breathe in the liquefied air, but I could still feel it rattling in my useless lungs.

Brady, however, was very much human and prone to sweating. He stopped wrangling with the equipment, and stood up, whipping off his T-shirt.

"Oh, my God," Patsy and I breathed together. We looked at each other, then at the glistening muscles of a half-naked Brady. I'd seen this view before, but I never tired of it. Brady was a hard worker, and smarter than everyone here—even Doc Michaels. But he wasn't the sort to shoot the shit.

He had a linebacker build—big, broad, muscled. His tanned skin was scarred with slashes and pockmarked with holes. Knives and bullets, I was sure—though I'd never asked. According to the rumor mill, he was a man who'd literally survived the slings and arrows of life, a life I could only guess at. But I knew a thing or two about surviving, and maybe that's why I admired Brady. And maybe, too, it was why he sorta scared me. I had a few scars myself, inside and out. Even though he'd never given me a reason to fear him—well, I had the kind of terrified in me that never went away.

We stepped back as Brady maneuvered the fifty-sixth pole into place. One hundred and thirteen of the five-feet-tall, six-inch-wide metallic poles would be installed around Broken Heart's perimeter. Calculations for where the poles needed to go had taken nearly as long to complete as making the darned things. I should know, since I was the one who had built the outer casings. All the whirligigs on the inside had been created by Brady and Doc Michaels. I didn't understand the technology, but I knew how to work with anything made of metal, and I could fix just about any mechanical device.

Part of my job was helping get the bugs out of the individual components; every single pole would have to play nice with the others to get the Invisishield up and running. Once it was operational, it would be as if Broken Heart had disappeared from Oklahoma's map.

"I've done my official freaking duty. My feet are

Excerpt from *Over My Dead Body*

killing me," said Patsy, rubbing her very pregnant belly. "I'm gonna be a cliché and go home to eat ice cream and pickles."

I laughed. Patsy was nearly eight months along with triplets. Having babies was a perk of being vampire and werewolf—you were kinda alive. She and Gabriel were the only loups de sang in the whole wide world—at least until their children were born.

Up until June of last year, Patsy had been Broken Heart's only beautician and I'd been the town's only mechanic. My role hadn't changed much, but Patsy had become queen of not only the undead but also the furry. Well, she wasn't quite official on that score. Even though the original seven Ancients had turned over their undead Families to Patsy's rule (not all willingly, mind you), the lycanthropes were a more traditional bunch. Broken Heart had been chosen to host the annual Moon Goddess festival, where Patsy would receive the official blessing of the priestesses. Then she'd have the additional headache of bossing around werewolves.

"Hey, there's my ride," said Patsy.

A white Mercedes glided over the field, stopping when it was next to Patsy. In the driver's seat was Gabriel. His moon white hair was drawn into a long ponytail framing his handsome face. He had the most amazing gold eyes, eyes that were only for Patsy as she maneuvered herself into the car.

"How are the shocks?" I asked, leaning in as Patsy strapped on her seat belt.

"It rides smooth as silk," said Gabriel. "Even off the road. It was amazing work, Simone." He grinned. "Too bad it's not dragonproof."

In February, their last Mercedes had been blown up by a pissed-off dragon. Now we had one living in Broken Heart—a woman named Libby. She was married a vampire named Ralph, who was daddy to the cutest twin toddlers. Libby and Ralph were gonna have the first dragon born in five hundred years. Needless to say, they'd been busy fireproofing their new house and everything in it.

I patted the side of the car and chuckled. "I'm working on it, Gabriel. One miracle at a time."

My gaze was drawn to Patsy's belly—three miracles in there, and almost ready to come out, too. I looked at Patsy and grinned. I was thrilled for her. She deserved some happiness.

"If the shield works, we won't need to worry about fireballs blowing shit up," said Patsy. "You take care, hon."

"You, too." I shut the door and off they went.

I watched the Mercedes wheel around and head toward the dirt road. Even though I wasn't exactly part of the town, at least not the way most folks were, I really did like the people here. But I'd also learned the value of getting too close to others—and I couldn't shake the habit of keeping to myself.

"Hello, my friends," shouted a German-accented voice. The man jogging toward us was Reiner Blutwolf. He was an old friend of our resident lycanthrope security detail, three gorgeous triplets that I really didn't have much to do with. Truth be told, they were even scarier than Brady, especially Damian. That guy almost never smiled. The closest he ever came was when he was around the jovial Reiner, who oozed charm.

I was probably the only one in Broken Heart who didn't buy his act.

"Hello, Simone," he said, flashing a blindingly white smile. What did he brush his teeth with? Bleach? Maybe he chewed on Greenies or something. Oh, now . . . that was mean.

I grinned broadly. Nobody could outjolly me. I had perfected the art of hiding behind bright smiles and perky attitudes. I could make Pollyanna look like the Grinch. "Hello, Reiner. You doin' all right?"

"I am, now that I've seen your smile."

Oh, puh-lease. His bright blue eyes were on mine and I looked away. I suppose some might call him handsome. To me, he looked like the ugly older brother of Brad Pitt. Finally I nodded my thanks for his lame-assed compliment, then pretended I wanted to get a better look at the pole Brady was wrestling into place. With my vampire strength, I could help easily enough, but so could the three other vamps standing around and watching him struggle.

"Would you like some help, Brady?" Reiner rounded the other side of the pole, stepping into my personal space. I didn't appreciate the subtle intimidation, and I scooted away.

Ugh. Reiner always picked me out of the crowd first, unless Damian was around. He reminded me of Roogie Roo, the old terrier owned by my friend William. I was allergic to dogs and Roogie Roo knew it, which was why he loved me. I couldn't resist letting that silly dog sit on my lap, even though I'd spend a full day sneezing and wheezing. In the same way, Reiner seemed to know I wasn't keen on him, so he tried extra hard to get my approval. Hah. I'd be damned if I let him onto my lap.

I brushed against Brady and stopped, startled that I'd gotten so close. His sweatslicked arm slid along mine, and if I'd had a heart, it would've skipped a few beats. I felt safer by him than I did Reiner, which was not a comforting thought. I glanced up at Brady, whose chocolate-brown gaze was on mine. His eyes narrowed; then he stepped between me and Reiner, clapping the man on the shoulder.

"I have a date," he said. "Maybe you and the bloodsuckers can finish up this one. I'll be back in a couple of hours to help with the others."

Excerpt from *Over My Dead Body*

"I didn't realize you and Simone were ... together," said Reiner.

I expected Brady to protest that I wasn't his date, but he merely smiled, picking up his shirt to wipe off his face. "Well, now you do."

I looked at the ground so that my shocked expression wouldn't give away Brady's little white lie. I'd much rather Reiner believed I was dating Brady—maybe he'd back off a little. Why was he so set on impressing me anyway? I was just a single mom who made her living working at a garage. I was nobody—and I liked it that way.

"C'mon, sweetheart," said Brady, tugging my hand into his. He threw the shirt over his shoulder and walked me to his truck. If I'd had the ability to blush, my cheeks would've been on fire. As it was, I couldn't look at anyone we passed. A few weeks ago, Brady had just up and offered to take me to the build sites and home again. I really liked his Ford Dually, which was as red as blood and rode like a wet dream. I'd caved, and now everyone would think it was because we were an item. Gah.

Brady opened the passenger-side door and helped me into the seat. Then he rounded the hood and got in. He pulled a clean T-shirt out of the glove box and tugged it on. Then he started the engine, flipped the air-conditioning on high, and backed the truck toward the road.

Most of the time we rode home in companionable silence, listening to country-western songs. We were both suckers for Hank Williams, Sr., and Patsy Cline. But he didn't turn on the CD player, leaving only the silence to thicken between us.

"What was that all about?" I blurted.

"What was what?"

"Announcing to Reiner—not to mention the rest of Broken Heart—that we are dating."

"Why? You got a boyfriend who might protest?"

He knew that I didn't, but that wasn't the point. I ached to ask him whether he wanted to date me, but I couldn't form the question. Who was I kidding? Say what you will about Brady; he was the protective type. I'm sure my reaction to Reiner made Brady put on his white-knight armor. How could he be interested in me? Nobody noticed me, not unless they needed something fixed.

"Look, Brady. I don't think we should tell people we're dating when we're not."

"Good point," said Brady. "How about I take you out tomorrow night?"

I turned to stare at him. My mouth opened, but no words came out. The truck hit a rut and we both bounced up. My head nearly grazed the roof. I grabbed hold of the door, and Brady chuckled.

"Relax. It's not like I can kill you."

An angry retort died on my lips. Everyone knew I didn't do anger. I was the most forgiving, sweet, kind soul you'd ever met in this life or the next. At least that was what I let people believe. Even before I'd been Turned into a vampire, I was second-chance personified. Not a day went by that I didn't remember or try to honor those sacrifices that had freed me from my old life.

ABOUT THE AUTHOR

Award-winning author Michele Bardsley lives in Oklahoma with her family. She escapes the drudgery of housework by writing stories about vampire moms, demon hunters, interfering goddesses, cursed wizards, and numerous other characters living in worlds of magic and mayhem. She loves to hear from her fans! Visit her Web site at www.MicheleBardsley.com or drop by the Broken Heart Web site at www.BrokenHeartOK.com.

Because Your Vampire Said So

by Michele Bardsley

When you're immortal, being a mom won't kill you—it will only make you stronger.

Not just anyone can visit Broken Heart, Oklahoma, especially since all the single moms—like me, Patsy Donahue—have been turned into vampires. I'm forever forty, but looking younger than my years, thanks to my new (un)lifestyle.

And even though most of my customers have skipped town, I still manage to keep my hair salon up and running because of the lycanthropes prowling around. They know how important good grooming is—especially a certain rogue shape-shifter who is as sexy as he is deadly. Now, if only I could put a leash on my wild teenage son. He's up to his neck in danger. The stress would kill me if I wasn't already dead. But my maternal instincts are still alive and kicking, so no one better mess with my flesh and blood.